BLIND SPOT

PAULA HAWKINS worked as a journalist for fifteen years before writing her first book. Paula was born and brought up in Zimbabwe. She moved to London in 1989 and has lived there ever since. Her first thriller, *The Girl on the Train*, has sold 23 million copies worldwide. Published in over forty languages, it has been a Number 1 bestseller around the world and was a box office hit film starring Emily Blunt.

Paula's second thriller, *Into the Water*, and her latest book, *A Slow Fire Burning*, were also instant Number 1 bestsellers.

BLIND SPOT

Paula Hawkins

PENGUIN BOOKS

TRANSWORLD PUBLISHERS
Penguin Random House, One Embassy Gardens,
8 Viaduct Gardens, London SW11 7BW
www.penguin.co.uk

Transworld is part of the Penguin Random House group of companies
whose addresses can be found at global.penguinrandomhouse.com

First published in Great Britain in 2022 by Penguin (Transworld)

A CIP catalogue record for this book
is available from the British Library.

ISBN 9781529176636

Typeset in 12/16pt Stone Serif ITC Pro by Jouve (UK), Milton Keynes.
Printed and bound in Great Britain by Clays Ltd, Elcograf S.p.A.

The authorized representative in the EEA is Penguin Random House
Ireland, Morrison Chambers, 32 Nassau Street, Dublin D02 YH68

Penguin Random House is committed to a sustainable
future for our business, our readers and our planet. This book
is made from Forest Stewardship Council® certified paper.

PART I

July

1

Jake Pritchard was dead.

His body, still warm, lay on the floor in the space where the open-plan kitchen met the living room, a halo of thick blood around his smashed skull. Still warm, but definitely gone.

Ryan Pearce knelt in the sticky ooze that seeped from Jake's terrible wounds. Ryan gripped his phone in his right hand. In his left he clutched a heavy glass object smeared with gore.

Ryan was still there, still kneeling, trembling and white-faced, when the paramedics burst through the front door. The medics quickly realized that there was nothing to be done for the man on the floor, the man with the glassy eyes and his head staved in. Instead they turned to Ryan.

Was he injured? they asked. What on earth had happened here? When had he arrived? What had he seen, what had he heard? Had there been anyone else in the house? Ryan shook his head but said nothing. He seemed unable to speak, unable to take in what was happening to him.

The paramedics spoke to him gently. With great care, one of them helped Ryan to his feet, removing as he did the glass object from Ryan's hand and putting it into a plastic bag. It had an engraving, the paramedic noticed, on its base: *Jake Pritchard, Best New Screenwriter, 2012.*

'Is this him?' the paramedic asked Ryan. 'Is this man Jake Pritchard?' Ryan nodded. 'Can you tell us anything about him? How do you know him?'

At last, Ryan spoke. 'I never meant to hurt him,' he stuttered, his teeth chattering. 'I would never hurt him. He's my best friend. He's my brother.'

2

Edie had slept late again.

She could tell, by the angle of the light pouring into the living room, as well as by the deep quiet of the apartment, that it was after nine. Such a luxury, to lie in, on Ryan's wide and generous sofa. Such a joy to sleep as she had, dreamless and undisturbed.

Here, in Ryan's small but beautiful one-bedroom flat, Edie was lulled at night by the noise of the city: teenagers laughing and drunks shouting, sirens in the distance and the comforting rumble of cars on the cobbled street below. The noises of community. So far from the loneliness of the house on the cliff, with nothing to listen for but the tortured cries of the gulls and the endless crashing of waves breaking on the rocks. It was shameful but true: Edie slept better on Ryan's sofa than she did in her marital bed.

Wriggling out of her sleeping bag, Edie shuffled through to the kitchen and popped a pod into the coffee machine. From the kitchen window she could see over the tops of the beech trees in the garden opposite to the park, and to the hill called Arthur's Seat rising above it. Her heart gave a little leap every time she stood here, surrounded by beauty and luxury. This was a world away from their shabby house on the cliff, their money worries, the slow-motion car crash of her marriage.

Back on the sofa in the living room, coffee in hand, Edie checked her phone. There were no calls from Jake, no messages either. She'd heard nothing from him in more than forty-eight hours. His silence was unusual, but, Edie realized with a sharp pang of guilt, not unwelcome. She'd heard enough from him lately.

She drank her coffee and was on her way to the bathroom to shower when the doorbell rang. Ryan, she expected, back from his run. He must have forgotten to take his key. She pressed the button to release the door downstairs and opened the front door. 'That was quick,' she called down the stairs, expecting to see Ryan come loping up the steps. Only it wasn't him. It was someone else. Two someones, in fact – two men in police uniform, their faces grave.

Edie's pulse started to race. 'What's going on?' she asked, reaching out to steady herself against the door frame. An incident, they said. Out at the cliff house. 'What happened?' she asked. She had an awful sick feeling, as though something slippery were moving around her stomach. 'Was there a fight?' she asked. The policemen looked at each other, surprised.

They took her inside, closing the door behind them. They sat her down on the sofa, standing opposite her while they explained why they were there. Her husband, they said, had been attacked in their home. He had suffered serious head injuries. Despite the efforts of the paramedics, they were not able to save him. He had been pronounced dead at the scene. It wasn't yet clear what had happened, but it looked as though it might have been a botched burglary.

For a few moments, Edie said nothing. She listened to the sound of their voices, waiting all the while to wake up. She dug her fingernails into her palms, pinched the skin on the back of her hands, and still the policemen did not disappear. She did not sit up, panicked, from a nightmare. She wasn't dreaming. This was real. This was happening.

'Where's Ryan?' Edie asked when at last she found her voice. 'What happened to Ryan?'

The policemen exchanged another of their looks. 'Ryan Pearce?' one of them asked, a deep frown creasing his brow. 'He's at the station. He's giving a statement. He's the one who found the ... who found Mr Pritchard. He dialled 999.'

'So, he's all right?' Edie said. 'Ryan's all right?'

3

For almost as long as Edie could remember, there had been three of them: Jake, Ryan and Edie.

She had met them at school, down in Sussex. Edie had just turned eleven when she moved with her family to be closer to the hospital where her little sister, Georgina, was being treated for a rare childhood cancer. When Edie thought back to that time, the word that came into her head was *abandoned*. Her parents were always elsewhere, consumed with anxiety over her helpless little sister who soaked up all their love like a sponge. Where Georgina was weak, Edie had to be strong. She had to be brave. She had to fend for herself.

And she did. Edie set aside her feelings of abandonment, put them out of sight and out of mind and just got on with things. She rode her bike to school. She made her own dinner when she got home. Sometimes, she even put herself to bed.

When she turned twelve, she started at a private school. Compared to the other children, Edie seemed grown up: she was serious, quiet and controlled. But the other girls in her class didn't see strength or self-reliance, they saw boring and stuck-up. They mocked her seriousness, and the more they mocked her, the more distant Edie became. She treated them with scorn, like the grinning idiots she thought them to be. She quickly found herself as lonely at school as she was at home.

Until, one day late in the summer term, she skidded in some gravel going down a hill on her way home from school and came off her bike. She was sitting in the dirt, picking bits of grit out of the scrape in her knee, when two boys came rushing over the top of the hill. She recognized them from school – they were in the year above, two tall, dark boys who the other kids stayed away from, for some reason. The pair of them hopped off their bikes, and the taller of the two held out his hand to help her up. 'Are you all right?' he asked. His smile was crooked, and he had a large, deep dimple on the right side of his face. He was the most beautiful thing she'd ever seen.

Edie gave him her hand. 'I'm Ryan,' he said, as he pulled her effortlessly to her feet.

The other boy, kneeling in the dirt to examine the wheel of her bike, said softly, 'I'm Jake.'

And that was it, the bolt of lightning, heart-stopping. Edie knew right away he was the one. From that day on, it was the three of them together, inseparable.

Only now there were just two: Edie, curled into a ball in the corner of the sofa, the floor around her littered with tissues, and Ryan, pacing back and forth, wearing out the carpet. Ryan was wild-eyed, manic, too jumpy to sit by her side, too wound up to do anything but replay that morning's terrible scene in his head and describe it to her.

'There was so much blood, Edie, I couldn't . . . *do* anything. I tried . . . I tried CPR, but it was useless. I mean – of course it was useless, he was . . . gone. And then I was covered in blood, just sitting there, and I said, he's my brother. And then they wanted to know why I lied, and I said, I didn't lie. I didn't *lie*.' Ryan shook his head. 'We used to say it all the time, didn't we? He's my brother. We're like brothers. I don't know why I said it. I don't know why I said it *then*. Christ, Edie, there was so much blood . . .'

Edie drew the breath deep into her lungs and balled her hands into fists. 'Ryan, please don't . . .'

'I'm sorry,' he said, looking at her for a moment. 'I'm sorry.' He fell silent for twenty seconds, thirty perhaps, and then he started up again. 'I waited in the car for a couple of minutes before I went in. I was just reading my phone, you know, just reading, just . . . Not doing anything really, just wasting time . . . just wasting time . . .' His voice cracked. He was going to say it again. She knew it. *If only I'd gone straight in. If only I'd just kicked the front door in instead of waiting, instead of walking all the way around to the other side of the house. If only if only if only.*

He'd told her his story what seemed like a dozen times: how he'd driven out to Jake's for their Thursday-morning run. How he'd been early, because the traffic was better than usual, so he'd killed a bit of time reading his phone in the car. When he went to knock on the door, there had been no answer, so he'd walked around the house to the cliff side. He'd seen that the sliding glass door was open, but he hadn't been worried, because Jake often left the door open.

The moment he'd stepped into the house, however, he'd known something was wrong. One of the dining-room chairs was lying on its side and there was a strange metallic smell in

12

the air. Ryan told her how he'd found Jake, lying face-down on the kitchen floor. He'd tried to turn him over, but it had taken one or two goes.

'There was so much blood,' he said. 'It was such a mess . . .'

'Please,' Edie said again, holding out her hand to him. Tears ran down her face. 'Please, don't.'

Ryan touched his fingers to hers and the contact seemed to bring him back to himself. He sank to his knees in front of her, pulling her to him. She could smell stale sweat under his cologne as he kissed the top of her head, her cheek, as he whispered into her hair, 'I'm so sorry, E. I'm so sorry.' He held her like that for a few minutes, and then he got to his feet and went into the kitchen. He picked up a bottle of whisky and two glasses and returned to sit beside her. He poured them both a drink.

'What are we going to do,' he asked in a quiet voice, 'without him?'

Edie shook her head. 'I just don't understand. I don't understand how this could have happened, how someone . . . *why* would anyone even be out there? It's miles from anywhere, and it's not like there was really anything to steal . . .'

Ryan shook his head. 'He shouldn't have

been alone,' he said, and Edie flinched. 'No, I didn't mean . . .' He looked crushed and grabbed hold of her hand. 'I didn't mean *you* should have been there. I meant *I* should have. I should have got there earlier. I just hate the thought of him being alone . . . It's always been him and me, you know?' Edie bit her lip. 'Thank God you weren't there, E. Thank God, because otherwise . . . I don't even want to think about what might have happened otherwise.'

Ryan drank his whisky and poured himself another. As he leaned over to top up Edie's glass, his face was unreadable – there was grief there, but guilt too. Ryan took a gulp of his drink. 'I feel as though we betrayed him,' he said. He wasn't looking at her, but Edie knew what he was thinking. He was thinking about all the time they had spent together over the past two weeks since she'd walked out on Jake. The two of them, sitting side by side on the sofa night after night, drinking wine and laughing at some nonsense on the television, her leg pressed against his, their eyes meeting every once in a while, her stomach in knots and his too, no doubt. Both of them knowing – without saying anything – that it could only be a matter of time.

'We haven't done anything wrong,' Edie said.

Ryan poured some more whisky. She wanted to reach for his hand, but she was suddenly afraid that he might resent her. He might even blame her for what they were feeling now. Her tears came again, and now they were not only for Jake, but for her and Ryan too. She was thinking that, from now on, Jake's ghost would always stand between them, his absence a constant accusation.

Edie woke with a start, her head pounding and her mouth dry. It took a second for her to remember, for the horror to wash over her once more. Jake was gone. Her husband was gone. And she was left with the memory of all the awful things she had said to him before she walked out.

It had been nearly two weeks ago. Jake and Edie were in the kitchen at home – at the house on the cliff. Edie was making dinner, Jake was re-reading one of his screenwriting books. They'd opened a bottle of wine and were racing towards the bottom of it, both of them already on their second glass.

As Edie stirred the sauce, she heard her phone buzz. She glanced over her shoulder: the phone was on the kitchen island, about two feet from Jake's elbow, a little too far away for him to read the screen. Edie saw him look over at it before returning to his book. About thirty seconds later, the phone buzzed again. Edie quickly reached across to pick it up.

She could feel Jake's eyes on her as she read the messages.

'Who is that?' Jake asked, his eyes back on his book.

Edie turned away from him, busied herself with the sauce. She paused a beat before replying: 'Lara.'

'Oh yeah?' His tone was cool. 'What's she want?'

Edie paused again. 'She's thinking about doing that ultra-marathon she talked about – you know, the Great Glen Run or . . . whatever it's called.' Edie turned to face him. 'She wants to know if I'll train with her.'

Jake looked up from his book. 'She wants to know if you'll train with her for the Great Glen Run or *whatever it's called*? Is that what she says in the text?'

Edie gave a big sigh. 'She just said the long run. We've talked about it before. I can't remember what the thing is called. Jesus! Do you want to read the message? Is that what you want, Jake?' Edie held out her phone. Her top teeth digging into her lower lip, she hoped against

16

hope he would roll his eyes and go back to his book. She prayed he'd be too embarrassed, too proud, to actually take the phone and look at the messages and see that they weren't from Lara at all. That they were from Ryan, who was asking how she was and whether she wanted to meet for coffee over the weekend?

But Jake wasn't embarrassed, and he'd lost all his pride. He held out his hand to take the phone.

'Yeah, all right,' he said. 'Let's have a look.'

Edie snatched the phone back as if scalded. 'For God's sake!' she snapped. There was no way she could tell the truth. That she'd lied because she knew he would overreact to her getting messages from Ryan, because he overreacted to everything these days. That she'd only lied because she was hoping for a quiet evening. Now, attack was her only line of defence. 'This is ridiculous, Jake! You're paranoid! You want to read my phone messages, now? You're *unbelievable*.'

'You offered the phone to me!' he yelled back.

'I was making a point. I was trying to show how crazy you're being. I would never ask to see *your* messages!' She shoved her phone into her back pocket, turning back to the stove and stirring furiously. 'Do you have any idea what it's like to live with someone who doesn't trust you?'

She heard the clatter of a stool falling behind her, Jake lurching to his feet. 'Do you have any idea what it's like,' he said, his voice dangerously low, 'to feel like the person you love is lying to you all the time? To watch their face every time they get a message, knowing they're hiding something from you? Never knowing where they've been, what they've been doing . . .'

'Oh my God!' Edie spun back to face him, tomato sauce spattering all over the floor as she waved the wooden spoon around. 'This is just *intolerable*. I'm a virtual prisoner in this bloody house, and you're complaining that you don't know where I am twenty-four hours a day? What has got into you? Where do you get these insane ideas from?'

The argument escalated from there. It ran along the usual lines, the same sort of argument they'd been having for months. Only this was the worst one yet. Him accusing her of lying to him, of betrayal. Her, furiously defensive, spitting curses at him, saying all the horrible things she thought in her worst, least kind moments, the things she never ever should have said. That he was crazy, paranoid, selfish. A failure. How she regretted spending all those years supporting him while he was writing. How she hated the cliff house, how she wished they'd never moved there, how all she wanted to do was to get away.

'So why don't you go then, Edie? Why don't you just leave? Go on! Go running to Ryan,' he said, 'like you always do.'

And so she did.

4

The sound of the coffee machine woke Edie a second time. Again, she felt a moment of peace, followed by a terrible surge of grief. As she reached for the box of tissues on the coffee table, she looked up. Her eyes met Ryan's. He was in the kitchen, dressed in suit trousers and a pressed white shirt, his tie hanging undone around his neck.

'Are you going out?' she asked.

He looked puzzled. 'I'm going to work, Edie.'

'But . . .' She pulled herself upright, gathering her sleeping bag around her. 'You can't. *Today? I mean . . . what about compassionate leave?*

Ryan's lip curled. 'Compassionate leave? Jesus, Edie, you can be naive sometimes.' He turned away from her. 'There's no such thing as *compassionate leave* in finance.'

Wounded, Edie wiped her eyes, swallowing the lump in her throat. She looked around at the mess she had created in Ryan's usually spotless living room, the empty glasses and the scrunched-up tissues, her jeans lying discarded on the floor. And she realized that he might not want her here. A few moments later, he came from the kitchen carrying two mugs of coffee. He placed one on the table in front of her and kissed her lightly on the head.

'Sorry, E. I shouldn't have snapped. I don't *want* to go in, but I already missed all of yesterday and there are clients to take care of. If I'm not there, someone else will step in, and that means I lose out. I can't afford that. That's just the way it is.'

The police came to fetch Edie at midday. Two more men in uniform, different ones this time, and a woman in plain clothes called Neeta Badami, who said she was the family liaison officer. 'Any questions, anything at all, you come to me, okay?' Neeta was young, in her early thirties perhaps, a tiny woman whose severe expression was offset by long eyelashes and a soothing voice.

Neeta explained that the police needed to take Edie out to the cliff house so that she could point out what, if anything, was missing. The police had found no laptop or mobile phone on the scene, so they were pretty sure those had been taken. But they were wondering if there

21

was anything else, anything distinctive, anything that might help them track the killer down.

Edie couldn't see the point. 'It's not like we had anything worth taking. You'll see. The furniture's all crap, second-hand mostly ... we didn't keep cash in the house, and it's not like we had any Picassos on the walls. I don't see why it's necessary for me to go all the way out there.'

Neeta gave her a reassuring smile. 'I know you don't want to go out there, Edie. I understand. In your shoes, I wouldn't want to go either. I've no doubt that it's going to be a traumatic experience, but I'll be with you every step of the way. There's a chance that this might be helpful for us, because you never know what a burglar might take. If they've taken something personal, that might help us track these people down.'

There was no point arguing. Edie allowed herself to be led to the car. She sat, silent and morose, in the back seat, staring out of the window. As they drove up on to the bridge, its lights blinking in the fog, she shuddered.

'Can you tell me,' Neeta said, sounding for the first time slightly unsure of herself, 'when you moved out of your home?'

Edie hugged herself, huddling closer to the

car door. 'Two weeks ago,' she said quietly. 'We had a row.' As she turned to face Neeta, she caught the driver's eye in the rear-view mirror; he was watching her intently. 'I'm being honest here,' Edie went on, 'because there's no reason for me not to be. We'd been going through a bad patch, having a lot of rows.'

'Anything particular causing the rows?' Neeta prompted.

Edie sighed. 'Money, mostly. In London, I'd been working as an executive assistant in a big firm. I had a decent salary. But since we came up here two years ago, I haven't been able to find anything permanent. I've just been working as a virtual assistant, which pays peanuts.'

'And Jake?' Neeta prompted again. 'Jake wrote for television, is that right?'

Edie shrugged. 'He did. Off and on. It's a difficult business, you know, to make regular money. My income was the one we relied on.' She wrung her hands in her lap. 'Jake had a few ideas rejected. He took that hard. It made him very frustrated.' She fell silent for a moment. 'We argued about the house, too.'

'What about the house?' Neeta asked.

'I hate living out there,' Edie replied.

'Really?' Neeta seemed surprised. 'But that stretch of coast is so beautiful . . .'

'But there's nothing *there*. Nothing going on – and I was stuck. Trapped. I can't drive, you see, because I've got this condition with my eyes. I have blind spots.'

'And yet you decided to buy a house out in the middle of nowhere?' the driver asked, sounding puzzled.

'We didn't buy it,' Edie said. 'It was inherited from Jake's father. I'd never even seen the place before we moved. Jake told me that it was in Edinburgh.' Edie gave a short, bitter laugh. 'I was so excited! And then we got up here, and I find it's not in Edinburgh at all. It's more than an hour's drive from the city – if you can drive, of course. If you can't, it's a bus and a train and it takes *for ever*. And it's on a cliff with no neighbours and it's a twenty-five-minute walk to buy milk.' She paused, taking a deep, shuddering breath. 'I hate it out there, to tell you the truth. I wanted to sell up, to use the money to buy something else, something in town. Jake said I was being selfish, expecting him to get rid of his father's home.'

In Edie's jacket pocket, her phone buzzed. She took it out and checked the screen: it was Lara calling.

'Do you need to get that?' Neeta asked, glancing at the phone screen herself.

Edie shook her head. 'It's a friend. I haven't even told her yet. I've hardly told *anyone* yet. Jake's step-brothers, my own family, but everyone else – friends, old work colleagues – I don't even know how to begin.'

Neeta reached for Edie's hand and gave it a quick squeeze. 'We can talk about that, if you like. I can help you.' She paused a moment before she added, 'I'm only thinking of this because you mentioned Jake's step-brothers. But I was wondering if you knew, Edie, why Ryan Pearce told the paramedics that he was Jake's brother? Did you know that he'd said that?'

Edie studied Neeta's face. 'Yes,' she said quietly. 'I did know. It wasn't a lie. If that's what you're thinking. He meant it . . .' – her voice cracked – 'he meant it in a good way. They talked like that sometimes, about how they were closer than friends, they were brothers.'

Neeta nodded thoughtfully. She looked out of the window for a second, then turned back to Edie. 'The other thing he said was that *he never meant to hurt* Jake. Do you have any idea why he'd say that?'

Edie looked down at her hands. She shrugged. 'I suppose because . . . by letting me stay at his place, it seemed like he was taking my side. And

25

that would have been hurtful to Jake. We both knew that, but Ryan was my friend too, so . . .' she tailed off. 'It was complicated.'

The car slowed as they neared the turn-off for the coast road. Edie felt her stomach lurch. She reached up and gripped hold of the roof handle as the car swung to the right. Her face felt hot, her breath was short. She could feel Neeta's eyes on her, the driver's too, both of them watching her as they headed towards her home. Both waiting to see what she'd do, how she'd react. It was like being an animal in a cage.

'Did your arguments with Jake ever become physical, Edie?' Neeta asked her.

Edie stared at her. '*What?* No! Are you . . . wait, what are you suggesting?'

'Not that you did anything wrong. We know from the CCTV in Ryan's building that you didn't leave the flat that morning, so we know you didn't do this. But we were wondering if perhaps someone who cared about you, who thought you were at risk, might have acted to protect you. They might not have intended things to go as far as they did . . .'

'You mean *Ryan*?' Edie almost wanted to laugh. 'You haven't been listening to me, have you? Ryan *loved* Jake, loved him like a brother. And, yes, Jake and I were going through a rough patch, but he would never have raised a hand to me. He just wasn't that sort of man.'

'What sort of man was he?' Neeta asked.

Edie smiled at her. 'He was loyal,' she said. 'He saw the good in people. He saw it in me. He loved me so much.' Tears began to roll freely down her face. Neeta fished a pack of Kleenex from her handbag and handed one over. 'He didn't like me being the breadwinner – that had always bothered him. He wanted to look after me – he was old-fashioned like that. He was stubborn. He was proud.' She blew her nose. 'He could be a bit of a dreamer. Head in the clouds.'

Edie wiped her eyes and took a deep breath. 'You need to slow down now,' she said to the driver, 'the turning's coming up.' As the car swung off the road on to a dirt track, Edie's heart rate started to rise. 'It's just along here,' she said. She was gripping the grab handle on the roof of the car again, her head bent and her chin to her chest.

'Are you all right, Edie?' Neeta asked. 'Are you feeling okay?'

'I'm fine,' she whispered. They were just passing the point where Ryan had picked her up on the night of the argument. She'd texted him while she was packing a bag: *Please come now, I can't stay here*. He was there in under an hour – he must have broken the speed limit all the way. As she'd climbed into his car, she'd turned back to look at the house: Jake was standing in the doorway, watching her. With the light behind him, she hadn't been able to see his face, but she could imagine it now, the pain on it, the hurt. That was the last time she ever laid eyes on him.

5

The first time Edie saw the house on the cliff, she said it looked like a public loo.

If you imagined a house on the Fife coast, you might conjure up a quaint fisherman's cottage, or something pleasing and modern in timber and slate. Jake's father's house was very different, a 1970s creation, a building so low-slung and plain that, as you approached it on the winding track from the main road, you hardly noticed it at all. There were no windows on the land side of the house, just a plain brick wall with a wooden front door. It wasn't so much ugly as utterly dull.

Until you stepped inside. The interior wasn't grand – it was shabby and tired – but the back of the house was entirely made of glass. Since it was perched no more than twenty metres from the cliff edge, when you stepped inside you saw the sea stretching out to the horizon.

Today, though, Edie's eye was drawn not to the water but to a dark stain marking the polished concrete floor. It was just at the point where the open-plan living room met the kitchen. Neeta stepped quickly in front of her, blocking her view. 'If at any time you need to take a break,' she said, 'just let me know.'

Edie gave her a curt nod. 'Let's just get this over with.'

Edie and Neeta shuffled towards the kitchen, awkward in their protective suits and plastic overshoes. They stepped around the horrible brown stain and stood underneath the kitchen skylight, once a dramatic feature, now marred by an enormous herring-gull nest. Edie looked around, opening and closing drawers and cupboards, checking the fridge. Everything seemed normal. She walked into the main living space. Opposite the wall of glass, its panes streaky with salt and grime, was an ugly stone fireplace, in front of which sat a tatty orange sofa. Ancient rag rugs lay strewn over the floor; the bookshelves framing the fireplace held a few dozen paperbacks and a few DVDs.

Edie stared at the shelves and then turned back to face the windows. She pointed towards the sliding door to the garden, which was open. 'Is that where . . . they got in?'

'We presume so,' Neeta replied. 'According to Ryan, the door was open when he arrived.'

Edie nodded. 'Jake left the door open all the time. He liked to hear the sound of the sea. And he said . . .' – her voice wavered a little – 'he said it was perfectly safe, because there was never anyone out here. It wasn't like anyone was going to wander past.'

Neeta took a few steps closer to the door. 'What about the coastal path?' she said, looking out at the patch of scrubby garden outside the house. 'Aren't there a lot of walkers out this way?'

Edie nodded. 'There are, but not this side of the house. About five hundred yards further south, a whole chunk of the cliff fell into the sea not so long ago, so there's a diversion now. The path runs inland for a bit, behind the house, up towards the main road. You can see the house from there, but you probably wouldn't really notice it unless you were looking for it.'

Neeta took a step forward, her nose very nearly pressed to the glass. 'Is it dangerous out there?'

Edie nodded again. 'When the tide's out you can climb down to the beach – over there, to the right, you can see the pathway. But you have to be careful, the tide comes in quickly. And every time there's a storm, a bit more of the cliff gets eroded. Won't be too long before this whole place slides into the sea.'

Neeta followed Edie along a corridor leading to the spare bedroom, which contained an old sofa bed and a small pine desk tucked into the corner. 'The office?' Neeta asked.

'Jake's writing room,' Edie said. 'Though to be honest,' she said, taking a few steps forward and placing her hands on the back of the empty chair, 'mostly he came in here to play on the Xbox.' She turned back to Neeta with a sad smile, brusquely wiping a tear from her cheek with the back of her hand. 'That's still here,' she said, pointing at it. 'The only thing missing is his laptop.'

At the end of the corridor was the master bedroom, furnished with a double bed, a couple of bedside tables and an ancient armchair piled high with clothes. The room seemed colder than the rest of the house. Edie sat down on the edge of the unmade bed and pulled the cover to her, clutching it to her chest and inhaling the scent of it.

Neeta stood quietly in the doorway, watching Edie cry. After a respectful pause, she asked Edie to look around the room again, to go into the bathroom, to check the wardrobes.

'There's nothing to take!' Edie exclaimed, looking miserably up at her. 'We didn't *have* anything; we were broke. Can't you tell from the state of this place? We don't have any art, apart from the cheap prints on the walls. We don't have an expensive sound system ... Everything is old and crap and second-hand...'

'What about jewellery?'

Edie held up her hand to show Neeta her wedding ring. 'That's it,' she said.

Neeta nodded. 'Jake didn't wear one, though?'

Edie frowned at her. 'Yes, he did. Same as mine, only his has my name engraved on the inside, where mine has his.' She slipped it off her finger and held it up for Neeta to look.

On their way back through the living room, Edie came to a sudden halt in front of the fireplace. She was looking at a space on the mantelpiece between a brass candlestick and a framed black-and-white photograph. 'The award,' she said, pointing to the empty shelf. 'Jake's screenwriting trophy, he keeps it there.' She turned to look at Neeta. 'It has his name on it. So that makes it pretty distinctive, doesn't it?'

6

Neeta was early.

Wrapped in a towel and dripping water on to the parquet floor, Edie opened the front door. 'You said ten!' she protested, standing back to let the police officer pass. 'It's not even nine thirty.'

Neeta smiled at her. 'I'm sorry,' she said, but Edie had the feeling she wasn't sorry at all. She suspected that Neeta had arrived early on purpose. Why, though? To catch her off guard? Six days after Jake's death, Edie was sleep deprived and still reeling from shock – she could never be sure when she was thinking straight and when she was being paranoid.

She left Neeta in the kitchen making coffee while she went to the bathroom to get dressed. But when she came out, she heard a noise further along the corridor, in the bedroom. Quietly, she padded along the thickly carpeted hall and pushed the door open. Neeta was over on the far side of Ryan's bed, looking at the framed photograph on the bedside table.

'I don't think you should be in here,' Edie said.

Neeta turned towards her. 'Sorry,' she said, smiling graciously. 'Just being nosy.'

Back in the living room, they sat, angled towards each other, on opposite ends of the sofa.

'What is it you wanted to talk to me about?' Edie asked her.

Neeta, though, didn't seem to be paying attention. She was looking around the room as though it was the first time she'd seen it. 'This really is a beautiful flat, isn't it?' She smiled at Edie again. 'I've walked along this road so many times and looked up at these places and thought, wow, that would be a place to live.' She paused. 'Expensive, I imagine.'

Edie nodded. 'Yes, I suppose. Ryan's in venture capital. He's done very well.' She followed Neeta's gaze around the room, took in the deep, jewel-coloured armchairs, the silk drapes at the windows, the art on the walls. 'And he comes from money,' she heard herself saying. 'He's always liked nice things.'

'So I see,' Neeta said, taking a sip of her coffee. 'Did that make things a bit . . . well, I don't know – a bit *difficult* between you? Ryan being so wealthy, while you and Jake were struggling?'

'Not really,' Edie said, turning her face away from Neeta for a moment. She pictured in her mind the day she and Jake had first visited Ryan in this flat, the look on Jake's face as he saw how impressed she was. 'We didn't really talk about that sort of thing.'

Neeta took another sip, then placed her mug back on the table and turned to face Edie more directly. 'Edie, do you know if Jake had debts? We know there was a small mortgage on the house, but apart from that – is there a chance he'd borrowed money?'

'A small mortgage?' Edie repeated. 'Right. Of course.' She'd had no idea. 'I don't think . . . No, we didn't have any debts. Any other debts.'

'Jake would have mentioned it if you had?'

Edie's face coloured. It must be obvious to Neeta that she hadn't known about the mortgage. 'I would have thought so, yes.'

'You're not sure?'

Edie sighed, rubbing her eyes with her fists like a sleepy child. She simply did not have the energy to be guarded. 'I told you,' she said, 'he was proud. And things were difficult between us, so . . .' she tailed off. She thought again about that last argument, when she'd called him a failure. Of course he hadn't told her he'd taken out a mortgage. Of course he wouldn't tell her if he'd had to borrow money! Why provide her with further failings to use against him?

Edie realized that Neeta was watching her, expecting her to say something more. 'The thing is,' she said, 'he'd done really well early in his career. He was barely twenty when his first screenplay got made – not for TV or anything. It was a little indie film, but it got into some festivals. He even won an award for it – the award that's gone missing.' She got to her feet. 'Actually, there's a picture I can show you. Ryan has one framed somewhere . . .'

On the bookcase next to the fireplace there were a number of small pictures in frames. Edie picked up one of them and brought it across to show Neeta. Taken the night the film premiered at the London Indie Film Fest, it showed a triumphant Jake holding his award aloft while Ryan leapt up, apparently trying to grab it from him. Handing the frame to Neeta, Edie found herself beaming through tears. 'They were so happy that night. Ryan was messing about, as usual . . . He always had this joke that the twist in the film was his idea, so he should have got some of the credit.'

'Is that right?' Neeta looked up from the photograph to Edie, one eyebrow raised. 'What was it about?' she asked, turning back to look at the picture. 'This screenplay.'

'It was about a man wrongly accused of a date rape. A kind of sexual politics thing, called *No Fury*. As in, hell hath no fury . . .'

'Like a woman scorned.' Neeta finished the quote, her eyes still on the photograph. 'What was the twist?' she asked.

'It's that he isn't wrongly accused at all. He just makes everyone believe he is. He gets away with it.'

Neeta looked up. 'That sounds pretty dark,' she said.

Edie looked away, suddenly uncomfortable under Neeta's intense gaze. 'Well, yeah, I mean . . . it was a creepy thriller. So of course it was dark. It was supposed to be dark.'

Neeta got to her feet, walked across to the bookcase and replaced the frame in its original position. She picked up another of the photographs and held it up to Edie. 'That's a lovely one of you,' she said with a smile. In the picture, Edie, Jake and Ryan sat on deckchairs in a small garden, all of them deeply tanned and grinning for the camera.

'That's our place in Streatham,' Edie said. 'We lived there just after we were married. It was this tiny little two-bed on the ground floor. All three of us were on top of each other all the time, but we were so happy there.'

'All three of you?'

'Ryan was living with us then.'

'Just after you were married?' Neeta gave her a strange look.

'Just for a bit. He'd . . .' Edie could feel herself blushing. She felt furious with herself. Why was she embarrassed about this? There was nothing *untoward* about it. 'He'd just broken up with someone, I think. I don't really remember the details. It wasn't for long.' She looked down at her feet. 'Anyway, we were very happy. The three of us.'

Edie could feel Neeta's eyes on her as the officer returned to sit next to her on the sofa. 'It must have been difficult, living on top of each other like that. I imagine there were arguments . . .'

Edie looked away. 'Not really.'

'Never?'

'Well, they were competitive, Jake and Ryan – they always had been, since we were kids. Who could run faster, climb higher, score more goals. When we were older, it was who had the fastest marathon time, who could do the most press-ups . . . boys' stuff.' Edie kicked off her slippers, tucking her feet beneath her as she slumped against the armrest.

'Nothing serious, then?'

Edie exhaled loudly through pursed lips.

'Why are you asking about this? No, they didn't argue a lot! When we were kids, maybe. Once, they stopped talking for a few months. Something about a camera – Jake broke Ryan's camera.' She could feel her face begin to flush again and turned her head away. 'Or something like that.'

Neeta shifted a little closer to Edie on the sofa. 'The reason I'm asking this, Edie, is because when the police officers came to tell you that Jake had been killed, the first thing you asked was whether there had been a fight. Now, you knew that Ryan had gone out there to the house, just like he did every Thursday morning. So I wanted to know – what made you think they would be fighting?'

Edie hauled herself back into an upright position. 'What *is* this, exactly?' she snapped. 'Are you questioning me now?'

'No,' Neeta said evenly. 'I'm just trying to understand why you thought that Jake and Ryan might have been fighting.'

'Why are we talking about this?' Edie asked. 'First you say you think it was a burglary, then you're asking about debts, now you're asking about Ryan . . . Are you saying you don't think it was a burglary any longer?' Edie could hear her own voice becoming louder, more shrill.

'Our first impression was that it was a robbery,' Neeta said carefully, 'but we're now six days into the inquiry and we haven't found any signs of a break-in. No locks were forced, no windows were broken, the TV and the Xbox were still there. We found Jake's wallet, containing sixty pounds in cash, in the inside pocket of his jacket.'

Edie sighed and folded forward, resting her forehead on her hands. 'But they didn't need to break in! The door was open. And maybe they just didn't find his wallet. What about the award? The one we were just looking at?'

Neeta cleared her throat. 'The thing is,' she started, and Edie could tell from Neeta's tone that she wasn't going to like whatever was about to be said. 'I didn't explain this to you before, because I didn't want to upset you, but the award isn't missing.' Edie gawped at her in disbelief. 'Our scene-of-crime officers removed it from the house on the day of the attack. We've been running some tests. We believe it is the murder weapon.'

'Oh, God.' Edie's face crumpled, and she buried her face in her hands once more.

'So far, the forensics team have found three sets of prints on it. Jake's and yours, and Ryan's, of course.'

Edie jerked her head up again. 'Why *Ryan's, of course*?'

'Well,' Neeta said, watching Edie's face carefully, 'we know that he handled the award. He picked it up, he says, when he moved Jake's body. In fact, he was still holding it in his hand when the paramedics arrived. He seemed almost . . .'

'Almost . . .?'

'Almost reluctant to let go of it, is what they said.'

7

Edie's phone shocked her rudely out of sleep.

She jerked upright, almost falling off the sofa. Bright sunlight shone in through the windows. She glanced at the clock above the fireplace – she couldn't have been out for more than fifteen minutes. Her phone stopped ringing. Then it started again. *For God's sake.* All she wanted to do was sleep. She reached over, picked the phone up off the coffee table. It was Lara again.

'Hello?' she answered.

'Edie!' Her friend's deep, throaty voice was filled with relief. 'At last. I've been so worried about you!'

'I know. I'm sorry, I—'

'No, don't apologize to me, don't be silly. Are you okay? Of course you're not okay. Can I come and see you?'

'Lara, I'm exhausted, I'm not sleeping . . .'

'Look, I'm going to come round and make you a cup of tea and then I'll sod off again, all right? I won't stay. Can I bring you anything? Food, drink . . .?'

Edie glanced at the almost empty whisky bottle on the top of Ryan's drinks cabinet.

'Bottle of whisky, Lagavulin?'

It was only just after four when Lara arrived, but Edie insisted on opening the whisky anyway. 'I've had a horrible day,' she said, moving miserably back to her nest on the sofa and pulling the blankets up around her. 'Being questioned by this woman, this *family liaison officer*.' She made quote marks in the air with her fingers. 'She's supposed to be keeping me up to date with what's going on, but I just feel like she's pumping me for information.'

Lara, impeccable as usual in a sharp black suit and bright red trainers, her dark hair scraped back into a high ponytail, settled into the armchair, her back to the windows. She leaned forward, elbows resting on her knees. 'But they can't think *you* were involved . . .'

'No, they don't. I'm not sure what they think any longer. First, they said a burglary, then they talked about debts, but . . . oh, I don't know. I'm not thinking straight. I *can't* think straight, I'm so tired. And I feel so bloody guilty all the time.'

Lara closed her eyes for a second. 'Because you weren't there, you mean? Because—'

'Because I was *here*. With Ryan.'

Lara said nothing for a few moments. 'When you say *with Ryan*, you don't mean . . .'

'Not like that, no. I just wish . . . I wish I could grieve in a natural way, you know? Just be upset in a normal way.'

Lara sat up straighter, giving Edie a sad smile. 'I'm not sure grief is ever natural. You feel what you feel. It's always complicated.'

Edie nodded. She drained her glass and leaned forward to pour herself another. 'Don't judge me,' she said, giving Lara a look.

Lara held up her hands. 'I'd be the last person on earth to judge you, Edie.'

Edie took another warming sip of the whisky, enjoying for a moment its pleasing numbing effect. She noticed now how, beneath her outward polish, Lara looked a little weary herself. 'Are you all right? You look a bit . . .'

'Knackered?' Lara smiled. 'Yeah, I've been working flat-out. I've had this big project I've been working on for ages. It's been a labour of love, but looks like it's all coming together at last.'

Edie nodded, relieved to have the focus of attention off her for a moment. She prompted

Lara to talk more about her company, Story-Time. It was a sort of podcast and audiobook business where people could subscribe to hear original stories, told over a number of days.

'The clever thing,' Lara said, 'is that you can also read the stories on a tablet or a phone, and then switch over to audio, depending on whether you're running or driving or sitting at home on the sofa. We've got all kinds – stories for walkers, stories for explorers, ghostly tales to tell around the campfire, stories for romantics . . . that sort of thing. Anyway, we're almost ready to test it on people. And then hopefully we'll have the real thing up and running in the autumn. I'll send you a link, if you like? A free trial.'

Edie nodded, then took another sip of her drink and sank a little lower into the sofa.

Lara cocked her head to one side, looking at her with concern. 'You're exhausted,' she said, picking up the handbag at her feet. 'I really ought to leave you in peace.'

'No,' Edie protested. The alcohol was making her glad of the company. 'Stay a bit longer. Tell me something else – anything. Are you still thinking of doing that ultra-marathon? Are you training?'

Running was Lara and Edie's common language, the thing they had bonded over in the first place. A month or two after Edie and Jake had moved to Scotland, Edie joined a running club as a way to try to meet people. She'd noticed Lara – tall, leggy and very quick – on her first run. Keeping her eye firmly on the London Marathon logo on the back of the tall woman's running top, Edie tried hard to keep up with her. She failed. But after the run, the tall woman – Lara – was the first person to say hello. She was open and friendly, if, Edie thought at the time, a little intense. She was Edie's first – and until Ryan moved up from London her only – Edinburgh friend.

Lara was chatting about her training schedule when Edie heard a noise outside and flinched. Lara stopped talking, her eyebrows raised. 'What's up?' she asked.

'Nothing, I just . . .' Edie was leaning forward on the sofa, craning her neck to see the front door. 'I heard something. I thought maybe . . .'

'Maybe?'

'Maybe Ryan had come home early.' Edie sat back on the sofa, still listening intently. She took another sip of her drink.

'Would that be a problem?' Lara asked her.

Edie chewed on a fingernail. 'He's not in a good way. I mean, *obviously* he's not in a good way. He's lost Jake, and he was the one who found him. But the way he's behaving, it's not . . . *normal*. He insists on going to work, insists that he can't take time off, but then he comes home and he's angry, touchy, almost . . . almost panicky? He jumps at loud noises. He flew off the handle when I slammed the front door by mistake a couple of days ago . . . I suppose it's like you said – everyone's grief is complicated.'

Lara nodded thoughtfully. 'Yeah, but it's not okay for him to get angry with you.'

'No, it's fine, it's *fine*,' Edie said miserably. 'But I do feel he resents me being here, that he'd really prefer it if I was somewhere else. And that's painful, because *I* feel as though we need each other more than ever.' She shook her head. 'I don't know – I'm overreacting to things, too. I'm too sensitive, I'm paranoid . . .' She drained her glass, leaning forward to pour yet another.

'Edie . . .' Lara bit her lip.

'You said no judgement, remember?'

Lara nodded again.

Edie leaned back again, crossing her legs in front of her, and took another large gulp. 'The thing about Ryan is that he doesn't deal with failure very well. He's not had much experience of it.'

'Failure?' Lara frowned.

'That's how he'll see this. He hasn't said as much, but I know Ryan – he'll be thinking that he failed his friend, let him down. And that he hurt Jake's feelings by taking my side, although that's not really how it was. It's just so complicated, all of it, and I just keep thinking . . .' Edie's voice cracked. 'I keep asking myself why. What have we done to deserve this? We're good people. We don't deserve this.'

Lara got up abruptly and went over to open the window. 'Stuffy in here, don't you think?' she said. For a few moments, she stood in front of the open window, looking out into the soft evening sunshine. 'That's better,' she said quietly, almost to herself.

Behind her, Edie drained her glass and settled down on the sofa, pulling the blanket up to her chin.

For the second time that day, Edie was jolted into wakefulness. No sunshine streamed in through the windows now. The room was pitch black. For a moment or two, she lay on the sofa listening to the frantic thump of her heart. She couldn't remember saying goodbye to Lara – she must have just fallen asleep. She remembered the whisky. She could feel the effects of it now, her head banging, her mouth dry. Throwing off her blanket, she struggled upright. Flapping frantically, she tried to find the table lamp to her left, but in the darkness she was as good as blind.

A wave of nausea swept over her, forcing her to sit still for a moment. Looking straight ahead without seeing anything, she started to feel that she wasn't alone, that there was someone else in the room. Perhaps Lara had fallen asleep here, too? Suddenly, she sensed movement, and in the next moment there was light. In the chair opposite her sat Ryan, his hand on the lamp switch, watching her.

'Jesus!' Edie yelped, shielding her eyes from the glare. 'Ryan, you scared me!'

Ryan didn't say a word. His face was blank, his eyes glazed. She realized that he was drunk.

'Are you all right?' she whispered. Still he said nothing. 'Ryan, what's happened? You're starting to scare me . . .'

'Your little friend,' he said at last, 'came to my office.'

Edie blinked hard, pushing her hand through her hair. 'My friend? What, *Lara*?'

He shook his head slowly, his eyes never leaving hers. 'Your other little friend. The policewoman. Her and a couple of her mates turned up at my office, virtually dragged me out of there. In front of the whole firm.'

'What? Why? Oh my God, Ryan, I had no idea . . .'

'Why? You tell me, E.' He didn't move, but his voice rose. 'You tell me why all of a sudden I appear to be the prime suspect in this thing.'

'*Prime suspect?*' Edie's heart leapt into her throat. 'No, Ryan, I didn't say anything, I didn't—'

'They wanted to know what Jake and I were fighting about that morning. They wanted to know whether we argued over Jake's film. Whether I envied Jake his success!' He laughed – a nasty, bitter sound. 'And then they wanted to know if we fought over *you*.' Ryan's lip curled into an ugly sneer. 'Is that what you told them? That we've spent all our lives fighting for your attentions?'

'Of course I didn't,' Edie replied, tears stinging her eyes. 'I never said that you fought over me. I didn't say that you fought at all. I mentioned the film, but only in passing. I don't even know why I was talking about it . . .'

Ryan got to his feet, swaying just a little as he did. 'No, I don't know either. But I do know this,' he said, as he started off in the direction of his bedroom. 'I want you to go.'

'*Ryan* . . .' Edie was starting to cry.

'Edie, I mean it.' He turned to face her and now the contempt was gone. There was no expression in his face. 'I don't want you here. Do you understand me? I don't want you around at all.'

8

After Ryan went to bed, Edie turned off the light and lay awake in the darkness, struggling to slow the beat of her heart. She must have fallen asleep eventually, because when she woke it was light and the flat was silent, still in a way that told her that Ryan had left for work. She got up, fetched a glass of water from the kitchen and took two paracetamol. She drew the curtains and found that the view had disappeared. The haar – a thick sea fog – had drawn in, blanketing the city in white.

She made coffee and returned to the sofa, noticing as she did an envelope on the coffee table with her name on it, next to a folded-up piece of paper. She picked up the paper first, unfolding it and reading the note:

Didn't want to wake you! Hope you get some proper sleep. I'll call you tomorrow xoxo.

Lara must have left it yesterday. She'd not noticed it last night, but that was hardly surprising, given what had happened. She picked up the envelope next. Inside was another note:

> *Sorry for last night. I was upset. I do think we need space to grieve?? Maybe best if you looked for somewhere else to stay for a while?? Rx*

Edie's spirits rose, only to sink again. She had hoped he'd have a complete change of heart – after all, where did he expect her to go? Not back to the cliff house, surely? She took a sip of her coffee and almost immediately felt a wave of nausea.

She ran to the bathroom, falling to her knees, clutching the toilet with both hands. She retched. Nothing came. She knelt there, desolate, hugging the bowl, sobbing quietly to herself, squeezing her eyes shut against her tears. When she opened them again, she saw something. A glimpse of metal at the bottom of the bowl. She plunged her arm into the water, her fingers closing around a small metal object.

For a few moments, she sat there on the floor, her heart pounding and water dripping from her arm. She was gawping in disbelief at the narrow strip of gold between her fingers, her own name engraved on the inside of the band. Jake's wedding ring.

This made no sense at all. Jake hadn't been over to Ryan's flat in weeks – not for a month, at least. It couldn't have been here all this time. Perhaps, she thought, the paramedics had given the ring to Ryan for safe-keeping. But then what? He'd forgotten about it? *He'd thrown it away?* Even in the state he was in last night, Edie struggled to believe that Ryan would have done that.

Her mind racing, she thought of the previous morning, of Neeta sneaking around, poking about in Ryan's bedroom. Neeta had used the bathroom – but what did that mean? That Neeta was trying to *frame* Ryan for Jake's murder? Or – Edie's stomach contracted into a tight knot – that Neeta was trying to frame *her*? Then again, Lara had been here too, hadn't she? She had used the loo, too. But how on earth would Lara have got hold of Jake's ring? Lara hadn't seen Jake in months.

She was being silly. She was being paranoid again. Wasn't she?

Sitting on the cold bathroom tiles, staring at Jake's wedding band, Edie became aware of a ringing sound, stopping then repeating, over and over. The doorbell. The postman, probably.

She was tempted to ignore it, but it continued, on and on, until she couldn't stand it any longer. She dragged herself to her feet, quickly washed her hands, splashed water on her face and went through to the hallway. She pressed the intercom.

'Edie?' It was Neeta.

Her heart banging against her ribs, Edie opened her mouth to say something, but found she had no words.

'Edie? It's Neeta Badami.'

'I can't talk to you right now, I'm—'

'Edie, can you open up, please?'

Edie took a deep breath. 'No, I can't. I'm not well, I—'

'Edie, we need to come and talk to you.' Neeta's voice was stern, like a schoolteacher. 'It's important. It won't take a minute, but it has to be now.'

Edie pressed the button to release the front door. She opened the door to the flat, her right hand gripping the door frame for support. In her left hand, she clutched Jake's wedding ring. She listened to their footsteps on the stairs. There seemed to be loads of them – it sounded like an army pounding up towards her. She felt a sudden urge to flee, but there was nowhere to go, nowhere to hide.

Neeta appeared, her face solemn, followed by

56

two officers in uniform. Not an army then, just three of them. Edie pulled her dressing gown more tightly around her. She swayed in the doorway, lightheaded.

'What is it?' she asked. 'What is it that's so important?'

'Can we just come inside for a minute?'

Edie stepped meekly back. The police officers walked past her, into the kitchen, where one of them placed something on the counter before moving away. Neeta took Edie's arm and led her into the kitchen. Edie pulled back against her, frightened, though she could not say of what. There, lying on the marble countertop, were two clear plastic bags, and inside them a mobile phone and a laptop.

'Do you recognize either of these items?' Neeta asked her.

Edie could feel her legs starting to shake beneath her. She nodded.

'That's Jake's laptop,' she said. 'The sticker – Warp Speed Films – that's his. The mobile . . . I couldn't say for sure, but it looks like his.' She felt Neeta's grip on her arm slacken. 'Where did you find these?'

'In the communal bin,' Neeta said, 'at the end of the road. One of the residents reported seeing them there this morning. They thought it was unusual for items such as these to be thrown away.'

Edie's head swam. 'The bin . . . just . . . just along the road?' Not fifty yards from Ryan's front door. 'I didn't put them there,' she said. 'I swear to God I didn't.'

Neeta nodded. 'No, we didn't think you put them there, Edie,' she said.

'Then . . . *Ryan*?' A sob caught in Edie's throat. She stumbled as her jellied legs started to go from under her. Somebody – one of the men in uniform, most likely – caught her before she hit the kitchen floor. The last thing she heard before she blacked out was the *ping* of Jake's wedding ring hitting the stone tiles as it rolled out of her hand.

PART II

November

9

And then there was one.

For almost as long as Edie could remember, there had been the three of them – Jake, Ryan and Edie. Before Jake, before Ryan, Edie was always alone. And now she was alone again: alone, and afraid.

The handles of her shopping bags cut painfully into her palms, as Edie walked the half-mile back from the bus stop to the track leading to the cliff house as quickly as she could. It was very cold and the light was starting to fade, her heart rate starting to rise. She had no night vision at all – she couldn't afford to be out after dark.

She had moved back to the house on the cliff a month ago. She'd had no choice: after Ryan was arrested and charged with Jake's murder, Edie had stayed on in his flat until his lease ran out. She certainly couldn't afford his rent, and her attempts to sell the house on the cliff had failed. There had been a handful of viewings, but no one had offered. *Try again in the summer*, the estate agent had said. *No one wants to buy a house in the dark*. No one wants to buy a lonely house on an eroding cliff whose most recent occupant was brutally beaten to death, was what he didn't say. But Edie understood.

For the time being, she was stuck here, alone in the ever-growing darkness. As the crow flies, the house was two miles from the nearest town, but once the curtain of night fell, it might as well have been on the edge of the earth. With wooded headlands both north and south, no other signs of life were visible, save for silently passing ships. No light and no sound, either – no drunken merriment or laughing schoolchildren. There was only the wind in the firs behind the house, the waves crashing against the rocks, the inescapable cries of the gulls.

Edie's troubles seemed inescapable, too. They were there on her doorstep as she shouldered open the front door – today's mail lying on top of yesterday's. Most of it would be bills she could not afford to pay. She stepped over the pile, turned on the lights and the heating and set about tidying away her meagre shopping. The rattling of air moving through the pipes set her nerves on edge.

Her groceries stashed away, she sat down at

the kitchen table and checked her emails, hoping for a reply to one of the job applications she'd sent out. But there was nothing – nothing but spam and marketing guff, including a message from StoryTime, Lara's company, offering her a free trial.

Edie snapped her laptop shut and steeled herself to deal with the physical mail. She sorted through the envelopes, setting the 'final demand' notices to one side. There was a letter from the courts, informing her of Ryan's trial date in three months' time. And then there was a letter stamped 'HMP Edinburgh'.

Edie had opened the first few letters Ryan had sent. She had read in every line his despair, his disbelief that she could possibly think him guilty of killing Jake. She'd agonized over his pleas for her to come and visit him and, after thinking it over, had set about arranging a visit.

That was when Neeta had intervened. 'Before you go to see him, Edie,' she'd warned, 'I think you ought to know the facts.' She said that the case against Ryan was strong, both in terms of forensics and motive. There were no other suspects. Ryan had tried to point the finger elsewhere. He'd made wild accusations against some mysterious woman whose name he could not recall. But there was simply nothing to suggest that anyone else was involved.

Neeta had presented Edie with a folder devoted to the case. The folder revealed, to Edie's horror, that she hadn't known Ryan at all. That she hadn't really known Jake, either. That the pair of them had been lying to her, betraying her trust, for years. It was as if they'd been living some parallel life of which she knew nothing.

First off, she'd had no idea how much debt she and Jake were in. Jake had been borrowing large amounts of money from Ryan regularly, starting way back when they first started having financial troubles. From the emails they'd been exchanging, it appeared that after Jake inherited the house, Ryan started asking when he was going to get some of his money back. Neither of them had ever mentioned any of this to Edie.

Nor had they talked about the fact that Jake had tried to dissuade Ryan from moving to Edinburgh in the first place. He'd written to Ryan saying that he and Edie 'needed distance' from him. He said that this was one of the reasons why they'd moved. Which, as far as Edie was concerned, wasn't the truth at all.

In another chain of emails, Jake referred to

'what happened with Tania' and 'the thing with L', and asked Ryan if he really wanted Edie to know 'the truth'. Edie had no idea what this meant. She knew who Tania was – she was an ex of Ryan's from a few years back. Theirs had been a messy break-up – Edie remembered the words 'crazy' and 'bunny-boiler' being bandied about. As for 'L', that could refer to any number of people. There was Lara, of course, whom Jake knew a little, but there were also a number of possibles among Ryan's many flings. Off the top of her head, Edie could recall at least two Lizzies, a Leanne and a Lucy.

After Neeta showed her the dossier, Edie had searched for Tania on Facebook but found nothing of interest: Tania had long since married and now just posted pictures of her children. Neither Ryan nor Jake had been active on social media. But Edie did discover a Facebook group of old pupils from their school, where the three of them had recently become the subjects of much discussion. Old classmates had posted links to news reports about Jake's killing, many of them including grisly details of the crime that had been leaked to the press. Even worse, beneath the reports about the murder and Ryan's arrest were dozens of comments, almost all of them nasty speculation and gossip:

Look at this! Can't say I'm surprised, those
  three were always weird
Ryan Pearce was a creep
Jake Pritchard was gay, lovers' tiff no question
Menage a trois gone wrong?
She got away with it didn't she?
Always was a stuck-up bitch
No way she wasn't in on it

Edie had closed the browser and hadn't looked at social media since. She had no interest in the lives or opinions of any of those hateful people. She and Ryan and Jake – they were better than them, they always had been. The three of them were a class apart.

But that was then. Now, as she got up from the table, tossing Ryan's unopened letter into the bin, Edie caught sight of her reflection in the window pane. Her pale face looked back at her, miserable and lonely as a ghost.

10

Edie left the house in darkness. It was danger-ous, with her poor eyesight, to run before sunrise. But she had little choice, since the sun only rose at eight in the morning at this time of year – and on some days barely seemed to bother to rise at all. She *had* to run. Running was the only thing keeping her sane. So she got up, laced her trainers, put on her head torch and set out in the dark, taking off through the trees, where wisps of fog snagged on black branches, hanging like spectres.

Back at the house, her limbs like lead, she was just about to get into the shower when her phone rang. She was tempted to ignore it – phone calls were never good news these days. But when she saw Lara's name on the screen, her spirits lifted. She answered. She listened to Lara chattering away. She was rushed off her feet on her latest visit to London, dashing from meeting to meeting, to her favourite hairdresser to get her colour done, to the optician to get new contact lenses. Then more meetings, and then possibly a date later on, though she wasn't sure he was her type.

Edie tried to respond in kind. She tried to keep things light, but found that she couldn't. She was ashamed to hear herself launching into a self-pitying speech about how lonely she was, how exhausted she felt. How she couldn't concentrate on books, and how watching TV made her more miserable still. It didn't matter what she watched, whether it was comedy or drama or a wildlife documentary, she found herself wanting to turn, as she always did, to Jake to discuss it with him.

Lara's voice was reassuringly warm. 'Do you know what you need, Edie? A companion. You should get a dog. There's a rescue place over—'

'I'm not a dog person,' Edie said.

'Well, they have cats, too. You can't run with a cat, of course, but they can be quite soothing.'

'I don't really like animals.'

'Okay.' Lara sounded disappointed.

'Not liking animals doesn't make me a bad person.'

Lara laughed. 'Of course not! Look, I was just trying to think of something that might cheer you up . . .'

'I was wondering about trying your podcast

thing. You know, one of your stories,' Edie said. 'I got a marketing email the other day – yesterday, in fact – and I was thinking, maybe listening to something might help me sleep.'

'Oh, yes – they're brilliant for that. Honestly, I've had loads of people tell me how relaxing it is, like having a bedtime story read to you. There's one . . . what's it called – oh yes, *The Main Chance.* It's a romantic comedy, funny and heart-warming. You should give it a go.'

That night, after her dinner of beans on toast, Edie took a warm bath, sprayed lavender on to her pillow, connected her phone to the speaker in the bedroom and clicked on the link for the story Lara had recommended. At quarter past eleven, she turned off the light and pulled the duvet over her, pleased to have something other than the waves and the gulls to listen to. The story *was* funny and the reader's voice was soothing. The next thing Edie knew, she was rolling over and looking at the clock on her bedside table and it was almost five a.m.

She had slept!

It was as close as Edie had come to experiencing a miracle.

11

Run, eat, sleep, repeat.

In December, darkness took over a little more every day. Edie's whole world seemed to encompass only the house, the woods and the coastal path – all of it dim, all of it grey. But she drew air into her lungs and ran further, faster – eight miles, nine, ten. She ran until she could barely stand. She wore herself out, so that at night, with the help of the stories, she slept.

Sometimes, she listened to the same story, over and over, finding comfort in hearing it again, in knowing that she didn't need to follow a new plot, only listen to a voice that would lull her to sleep. Sometimes, the stories ran into one another while she was sleeping. Sometimes, she fell asleep listening to one voice, and woke to another.

That was what happened to her one night in early December: she fell asleep listening to an American man telling a funny story of a family living in the Californian countryside, and woke, in the early hours of the morning, to something quite different. A woman's voice telling a different story, setting a different scene. Describing a lonely house, backed by a stand of trees, a modern house of grey stone and concrete, with a wall of glass facing the sea.

Edie's heart rate ticked up.

The voice described an open-plan living area, the stone fireplace in the living room, the skylight in the kitchen, on top of which a herring gull had made its nest.

Edie jerked upright in bed. She made a lunge for her phone, missing and sending the bedside lamp crashing to the floor. She grabbed the phone, swiping desperately at the screen to unlock it, while the voice kept on, describing the crumbling cliff face at the bottom of the garden . . . At last, Edie managed to close the app. The voice fell silent.

For a few moments she sat stock-still, clutching her phone to her chest. Beneath the skin of her wrist, her pulse fluttered like a trapped bird. Her mind racing, she was veering towards the edge of panic. She took a deep breath and reminded herself that this house used to be rented out. Every summer, Jake's father had gone abroad, and while he was gone the house was let to tourists. Also, he must have had friends, visitors. And then there were the people who had viewed the house when she'd tried to sell it . . .

Edie managed to calm herself, to reassure herself that she was overreacting. Sure, it was creepy, but it was just chance, a coincidence. Feeling a bit foolish, she hopped out of bed to pick up the lamp, climbed back in and re-opened the app. The story she'd been listening to was called *A Special Place in Hell*. The writer was credited by their initials only: GAL.

Leave it alone, Edie thought. *Switch it off, listen to another story.*

She couldn't leave it alone.

She pressed play.

It's a warm July day. The sliding glass door which gives out on to the cliff is open. The scent of the sea, the tang of salt and seaweed drift up to the house. Inside, the ringing silence of a space recently occupied and now empty. A place once full of life, now a void. On the floor lies a man. Or what used to be a man but is now a body. Blood still leaks slowly from the wound in his head, the split in his skull where a heavy glass object has been brought down on it with great force.

She was dreaming. That was what this was – it had to be. She was in the middle of one of those hyper-real nightmares you sometimes have, when you dream that you have woken, only to find that strange things are happening. The sort of dream you have when you know you are dreaming and you have to fight to wake yourself.

Only she couldn't wake herself.

She sat in her bed with the light off and her eyes fixed on the window in front of her, on the nothingness outside, and listened to a voice telling her a story she already knew.

The story was about revenge.

In the first episode, the scene is set: Rosie is a clever girl who passes an exam so that she pays no fees at a private school in rural Sussex. She is beautiful and bright and bullied because she comes from a poor, chaotic family. Povvo, they call her. Pretty povvo! As she gets older and prettier, Rosie gets more and more attention, most of it from boys. The attention is different now and Rosie accepts it as though it is generously given, which it is not. There is graffiti all over the toilet walls about Rosie, about what Rosie does and where and with whom.

Three of her classmates do not join in the

bullying. These three – Michael, Josh and Ellen – hold themselves apart. They are a closed circle, a little clique separate from the rest. But one of the boys – the handsome one, Michael – has started to take notice of Rosie. He smiles at her as he passes her in the corridor, and the smile is not just a leer. It is something else. She thinks he might be different.

One weekend, there is a party at a classmate's house, and Rosie plucks up the courage to go. She endures the snide remarks about her cheap clothes and her Primark earrings, numbing herself with vodka. When the gang of three turns up, Rosie says hello. Ellen ignores her, stalking off to sit somewhere alone, but the two boys stay and talk. They drink more vodka. At some point, they decide to go and explore upstairs. They find their way into a bedroom. Someone takes off Rosie's top, pulls up her skirt, pulls down her knickers. Starts taking photographs.

No one believes that Rosie – *pretty povvo* – did not consent to all this. Her claims of assault are quickly dismissed as fantasy, especially when Ellen backs up Michael and Josh's story, swearing that the boys were never alone with Rosie.

Now Rosie is not just poor. She's not just a slut. She's a liar, too. And so the bullying gets worse – worse still when pictures of her, drunk and dishevelled, her flesh on show and her face a grimace, are shared around the classroom. Crushed and shamed, Rosie stops going to classes. She stops eating. She drinks half a bottle of vodka and takes some pills to go with it.

Mercifully, Rosie recovers. She is saved, first by paramedics and then by a good therapist and a new school and a kind teacher. She remembers that she's not just pretty, she's clever, too. She gets her A levels, goes to university, casts off her trauma like a snake shedding its skin.

Until one day, fifteen years and hundreds of miles from the night of the party, Rosie sees *him*: Michael. He looks just the same, tall and handsome, swaggering along the street. She watches him walk into a bar, cross over to a table, and there they are – Josh and Ellen, too. All three of them, together and carefree, hugging each other, laughing, living their happy, blameless lives. A wave of pure fury, long suppressed, washes over her, and she decides: this will not last.

Episode two: in the middle of the night, Rosie drives to the remote house where Josh now lives with Ellen. Knowing that Ellen is away on business, she breaks in and murders him, savagely smashing his skull with a heavy glass vase. Then she sets about the tricky task of framing Michael. And once Michael is behind bars, she sets her sights on her final target, the real prize: Ellen.

Frozen with fear, almost too terrified to move, Edie's finger hovered over the link for the third episode, ready to click on it. Surely she will wake soon? Surely this must end? Her heart battering her ribs, she pressed on the link. The phone made a chiming sound and a message popped up: *Episode three of this story will be released on December 8th! Thank you for listening!*

Edie closed her eyes, flooded with relief. She didn't have to listen. She didn't have to find out how the story ended. Her phone vibrated in her hand and she jumped. She looked at the screen. There was a text message from an unknown number:

WHAT HAPPENS NEXT?

12

By the time the sun began to rise over the sea that morning, Edie's bed was strewn with papers, cards and photographs. They were mementoes of her childhood and teenage years that she had fetched from the shoeboxes stashed at the bottom of the wardrobe. In her fingers she held the earliest picture she could find of herself with Jake and Ryan. The three of them were standing astride their bicycles in the driveway of Jake's parents' house. They were wearing shorts and T-shirts, squinting into the sun. They must have been around thirteen.

Edie looked at the photographs and she felt full, overwhelmed with love for them and the pain that had come to choke it. She checked her phone for what seemed like the five-hundredth time, to see if there were any further messages. To see if Lara had replied to her texts, sent hours ago in the middle of the night, asking her to call back as soon as possible.

She checked the time, too. How early was too

early to call Neeta Badami? She had to tell her Ryan was innocent! This proved it! This story was a *confession*.

The problem with calling Neeta was this: the details of the murder were known to the public, thanks to leaks to the press. And it was possible that whoever had written this story might have visited the house as an Airbnb guest or a potential buyer. The real problem was, it wasn't the details of the murder that proved the truth of the confession: *it was the earlier part of the story*.

Because there *was* a party, when they were teenagers. That was true. And there was a girl, blonde and big-boobed, a girl with a reputation. She'd worked her way through most of the boys in the year above. And then she'd set her sights on Ryan, following him around all the time, batting her lashes. Edie couldn't stand her. The girl came to the party. She threw herself at Ryan. Afterwards, she made up a story about how Ryan and Jake had led her to a bedroom and taken advantage of her. Taken pictures of her.

When, at lunchtime on the Monday after the party, Edie was summoned to the head teacher's office to give her version of events, she told a white lie. She said she'd been with the boys all night. It wasn't the truth, but it might just as well have been. Ryan didn't need to *take advantage* of some girl. He had girls throwing themselves at him all the time. And Jake only had eyes for Edie. They were both innocent.

The slutty girl left the school a few weeks after the party and they never heard of her again. Edie had never thought of her again. Now, as she sorted through papers and photographs and mementoes from her school days, she could not find a single photograph of the girl, not a single mention of her in the school magazine. And though she tried hard, Edie couldn't remember the girl's name.

But she did know one person who she was pretty sure would never have forgotten.

Ryan.

13

What would people think, Edie wondered, if they could see her now? If they could follow her as she shuffled through prison security, clammy hands shaking, eyes firmly on the ground before her. Now raising her arms for a body search. Now her heart pounding because she would soon see, for the first time in months, the man accused of splitting open her husband's skull?

Would people assume, like her former classmates on Facebook, that she was *in on it*? Is that what Neeta would think? Edie hadn't spoken to Neeta yet – not about the podcast story and not about this visit. She'd decided that she needed to speak to Ryan first.

After the lockers, Edie and the other visitors – the sad-faced women, the mothers and daughters and wives and girlfriends whose men had failed them so terribly – were shown into the visitors' room. Edie looked around. She felt out of place in such company. She had to keep reminding herself: *I'm not like them. I'm different. Ryan hasn't let me down. Ryan is innocent.*

By the time the prisoners were shown in, Edie was fizzing with adrenaline. And when she saw him, she thought her heart might explode. His handsome face was haggard and pale. There were patches of grey in his beard that hadn't been there before. As he came closer, she saw that he had a cut across his left cheekbone, and around his left eye was the tell-tale green tinge of an old bruise.

He smiled at her, that familiar crooked smile, and her heart flipped.

'You look tired, E,' he said, cocking his head to one side as he took the seat opposite hers. For a few moments, Edie couldn't speak. She stared at him, her lips slightly parted. 'Ah, come on,' he said. 'Surely I don't look that bad?'

She shook her head. 'Are you . . .' Her voice came out as a croak and she coughed. 'Are you all right?'

'Better for seeing you,' he said. He held out a hand across the table. Edie, frozen with emotion, didn't take it, and so he carefully withdrew it, folding his hands together on the table. He was silent for a few moments. Then he looked up, his expression hopeful. 'I thought you'd given up on me,' he said. Edie thought her heart might break. 'Do you know the trial is in three months? Just three months . . .' He looked around the room, and when his eyes met hers again, she could see they were wet. 'I didn't do this. You know that. You know that I *couldn't*, Edie.'

'Yes,' Edie managed to say at last. 'I know that. I believe that now.'

Ryan bowed his head and his shoulders started to shake. 'I can't tell you,' he managed to say, 'how much this means to me.'

Edie watched him for a moment, pressing her fist to her lips to keep from sobbing. 'I do believe you,' she said after a few moments, 'but I don't understand why you kept things from me, why you lied to me . . .'

'We weren't lying,' Ryan said, looking up at her, pushing one hand through his hair. 'Look, E, it was stupid stuff – stuff you didn't need to know about—'

'Stupid stuff?' Edie hissed, eyes wide. 'It was thousands and thousands of pounds, Ryan! I don't even know where any of it went – he certainly didn't spend it on me, or the house, or . . .' She spread her hands in confusion. 'What did he do with it all?'

Ryan looked off to one side for a moment before meeting her eye again. 'He enrolled in that screenwriting course. Remember, the one you said you guys couldn't afford? He was trying to better himself, trying to get back in the game . . . He also made some investments. Bad ones. I tried to tell him that you should only go in for the exotic stuff if you can afford to lose money, but he wouldn't listen. He didn't want to be told. Certainly not by me.'

Ryan leaned forward over the table, keeping his voice low. 'He was ashamed, okay? Jake felt ashamed that he kept having to borrow money from me.' He sat up straight once more. 'I argued with him – I said he shouldn't keep it from you, but he wouldn't hear of it. He didn't want to look small in front of you. So I went along with it.' He reached out a hand for hers again and this time she took it, his touch sending a jolt right up her spine. She could feel her face flushing and she looked away. 'We've always supported each other, haven't we? Edie? Look at me. We've always backed each other up.'

For a long while, Edie said nothing. When her eyes finally met his, she asked, 'Do you remember that girl at school, Ryan, the one who said you assaulted her? The one people used to call Povvo?'

Ryan leaned back in his chair, a frown on his face. '*What?*'

'You don't remember?' Edie prompted. 'I was fourteen, so you and Jake must have been fifteen. We went to that party—'

'Yes, I remember *that*,' Ryan interrupted. 'Of course I remember that! She said I *raped* her,' he hissed. 'You don't forget things like that.' A look of disappointment crossed his face. 'Why are you asking me about that?'

'I can't really explain all this now. We don't have a lot of time, but it's important for me to find out about that girl. I need to know, do you remember her name?'

Ryan breathed out a quick sigh. 'Louise,' he said. 'Her name was Louise Grant.'

Louise Grant. That was it! Hearing her name brought back a clear memory of the three of them – Jake, Ryan and herself – standing outside the school gates on the Monday lunchtime after the weekend of the party. Ryan had his arm around Edie's shoulders. Jake was leaning against the fence, a cigarette cupped in his hand, misery all over his face. 'That girl, Louise,' Ryan was saying to Edie, 'she's saying all kinds of stuff about us. About how we attacked her, how we did stuff to her.' Ryan's eyes were huge, his tone pleading. 'You have to help us, E – we could be in real trouble.'

Edie remembered looking from Ryan to Jake,

but Jake's face was turned away from hers. 'You know us,' Ryan went on. 'You know we couldn't do something like that. You have to tell them, E. You have to tell them it's not true.'

Edie looked at Ryan now, at the bruise around his eye, at his hands, nails bitten to the quick. She would have done anything for him then, and she would do now. And yet, in the back of her mind, a thought snagged. 'Ryan, there's just one other thing.'

'Time's almost up, Edie, and I need—'

'Someone saw you,' Edie interrupted him. 'On the day Jake died, some guy out walking his dog saw you park your car outside the house twenty minutes before you told the police that you got there.'

'I thought you said,' Ryan's voice rose, 'that you believed me?'

'Why did you lie to them? What were you doing for those twenty minutes?'

Ryan leaned forward, putting his elbows on the table and massaging his skull with the tips of his fingers. He took a deep breath. 'Jake and I had an argument, a day or two before I went over there. We hadn't spoken. I wasn't even sure if he was going to let me in. I was thinking about what I was going to say to him.'

'What argument? You never told me that. I

was staying with you at the time, Ryan. Why wouldn't you tell me about an argument?'

Ryan shook his head and looked worried. 'Because the argument was about you,' he said.

Edie's face flushed. 'What do you mean?' She was embarrassed, but she was pleased, too. She'd never been able to shake that – the feeling of pleasure she got from their competing over her.

Ryan met her eye, noting her expression, her embarrassment. He looked away. He was embarrassed, too. He was embarrassed *for* her. 'I didn't mean the argument was *over* you, Edie. It was about you.'

Edie's blush deepened. 'Yeah, all right. How do you mean, *about me*?'

'I wanted him to be honest with you,' Ryan said, his eyes meeting hers before sliding away. 'About the woman he'd met.'

Edie heard a rushing sound in her ears, like the sea, like the wind in the pines behind the house. She felt as though the ground beneath her were tilting. She clutched the table top with both hands.

'*What?*'

Ryan sighed. 'He was seeing someone, Edie. I saw them together, in the bar at the Balmoral. They were . . . well, it was obvious they were together. He lied about it, of course. He said she

86

was a producer, but I could see he was lying – he was so sneaky about her, he got so angry.'

For a moment, Edie was speechless. 'But . . .' she spluttered at last, 'why wouldn't you tell me that?'

Ryan looked at her, then turned his palms upwards. 'How could I, E? I couldn't have done that to him, or to you. And you'd never have believed me anyway. You always had a blind spot when it came to him.'

'But . . .' Edie was baffled. 'How could he have even met someone? He barely ever left the house.'

Ryan gave her the saddest smile. 'He met her through you. I can't remember her name. Lorna? Laura, maybe? Some woman from your running club.'

'*Lara?*'

'Yes, that's it. Lara.'

14

There was a storm coming.

A red weather warning, it said on the news. Heavy rain was forecast, with winds of fifty miles an hour, gusts up to eighty. Let it come, Edie thought to herself as she got off the bus that afternoon. Darkness was already gathering. Wind was whipping fiercely off the sea. Let it come. Let it tear the house down, wash the whole rotten place out into the sea.

Like a whirlwind herself, Edie tore through the house, searching for signs of what Ryan had told her. She ransacked Jake's office, dumping the contents of his desk on to the floor. She pulled his clothes from the wardrobe, sniffing the collars for a whiff of some alien perfume, but finding only the faint scent of him. She inspected his coats for tell-tale long dark hairs. She went through his pockets for damning receipts. She found nothing.

Lara? Jake and *Lara*? It wasn't possible, was it?

Edie called Lara's number a dozen times. She

left a dozen messages. *Please call me. It's urgent. Lara, I really need to speak to you.* She racked her brain, trying to think of all the times she had seen Jake and Lara in the same room. There weren't many. They had all met in town for a drink once. They ran a half-marathon together last year, and after that, Lara had come out to the house for dinner. They had all had much too much to drink. Jake had gone to bed early, leaving the two of them sitting outside, fighting off the midges. That was it.

Wasn't it? Edie thought about Jake's moods in the few months before he died – his paranoia, that strange jealousy, his response when she said she'd got a text from Lara. Was that all some sort of twisted reaction? Maybe he was behaving strangely not because he *didn't trust her*, but because he was *feeling guilty*.

She slipped her favourite coat of Jake's over her shoulders and, wrapping it tightly around her body, wandered miserably back through the house and into the kitchen. On the counter sat a clear plastic bag containing Jake's laptop. The police still had his phone, but they had returned the laptop a couple of weeks back. Edie hadn't even opened the bag. Now, as she looked at it, adrenaline started to move through her system once more.

If there were any signs of an affair, they would be on the computer, not hidden away among phone bills and rejection letters from television networks. If she really wanted to know what was going on in Jake's life towards the end, the computer would be the place to look. The question was, *did* she really want to know?

After a few attempts, she figured out his password – the date of their wedding. Ironic that he would choose that date, when they had exchanged vows, to hide signs of a mistress.

But if there were any signs, Edie couldn't find them. There was nothing in his emails – no messages to or from Lara, or any other mystery woman, for that matter.

Edie opened his work folder, skimmed through his ideas for series, his half-written pitches for television networks. In a folder titled 'PICS', she found scans of their wedding photographs. There were also pictures taken on a holiday in Italy with Ryan a few years ago, and some of picnics in the park near their old place in London.

In a sub-folder titled 'PICS1', she found a folder called 'L'. Edie's heart sank. Steeling herself for something seedy – pictures of Lara in her underwear or, worse, a video – she opened the folder. There were just two files inside. The first *was* a picture of Lara, but hardly a sexy one.

It was Lara after she'd run the Edinburgh half marathon last year, flanked by Edie and Jake – all three of them red-faced and sweaty, grinning for the camera.

The second photograph wasn't of Lara at all. It was an old school photograph of the athletics team. If you squinted hard you could make out Edie in the front row, her hair cut into a severe bowl. Behind her, in the second row, Ryan and Jake stood side by side, arms folded across their chests.

Edie closed the file. She got up to put the kettle on, her mind racing all the while. Something was bothering her, something about that image. She went back to the computer and opened it again. She leaned forward and zoomed in to enlarge the image. There! In the front row, two or three faces down from where Edie sat, was a pretty, blue-eyed blonde. *Louise.*

In her jeans pocket, her phone began to vibrate. She fished it out and looked at the screen. A text message, from an unknown number.

HAVE YOU FIGURED IT OUT YET?

And then another:

WHAT HAPPENS NEXT?

A jolt ran through Edie like an electric shock. She opened the first picture again. She looked from Lara, with her luscious dark hair, her green eyes, her toned arms, to blonde, curvy, blue-eyed Louise. *No.* It couldn't be. There was a rushing sound in Edie's ears. She felt as though she were falling. She stared at the picture of Lara, who had to go to London at least once a month because there was only one colourist she trusted with her hair. Lara who wore contact lenses. Lara who had once owned up, towards the end of an evening in the pub, that she'd been chubby as a teenager and had to work hard to look the way she did now. Lara and Louise, sitting side by side in a folder that Jake had created and named 'L'.

Edie's phone buzzed twice. She stared at it, almost too frightened to pick it up. There were two more messages from the unknown number. She clicked on the first one. It was an image. It took a second to download. Then she saw that it was the school photo again, but in this version Jake's face had been crossed out. Ryan's, too. The second was one sentence:

There's a special place in hell for women who don't help other women.

Edie dropped the phone as if scalded, and the moment it hit the table it started to ring, the vibrations causing it to spin. She backed away, too terrified to answer, cringing as an almighty crack of thunder shook the house. She reached out and picked up the phone, pressing it to her ear. She could hear breathing. But for a moment she wasn't sure if it was on the other end of the line, or her own. Then a woman's voice spoke:

'So, have you figured it out yet? Come on, tell me! What happens next?'

15

The storm was raging. The wind was hurling handfuls of rain and sea spray at the windows of the house. From the stand of trees behind there came a howling, as though branches were bending to breaking point, as though trunks were being ripped from the earth.

When the wind dropped for a moment, Edie spoke. 'Louise?' she said, pressing the phone against her ear. She walked quickly along the corridor, fear prickling her spine. She ran into the bedroom and climbed into bed, pulling the duvet over her. 'Louise?' she said again. 'Is that you?'

'Call me Lara,' the voice said. 'I've not been Louise for twelve years. I changed my name after I was released from hospital.' She paused. In the silence, Edie heard the *click, hiss* of a cigarette lighter. 'I was ill. I don't know if you knew that? Well, now you do, because I wrote about it in the story. I tried to kill myself, so I was sectioned.'

She paused again. 'Did you like the story?'

Lara's voice was weirdly upbeat, as though she were enjoying herself. 'I thought it was pretty good for a first attempt at fiction. Or would you call it non-fiction? Whatever. The earlier parts pretty much wrote themselves, but the bit I'm having trouble with is the ending. I was thinking you might be able to help out with that.' She laughed, a brittle sound that sent a shiver along Edie's spine.

'What do you want, Lara?'

'I want to get it right! I've been working on this for the best part of two years now. It's been quite the labour of love.'

'You've been planning it since we met?'

'Since we *reconnected*. Before that, I was just getting on with my life, letting the past stay in the past. I'd had to deal with so much misery and so much hurt. But I'd got myself to a good place – setting up the business, moving to a new city, a place that wasn't tainted with bad memories. And then, one day I go to meet my running club and there you are, like some demon who's followed me up from hell. Edie Easton—'

'Edie *Pritchard*.'

'Yes, of course. Edie Pritchard, who married her childhood sweetheart. One of her childhood sweethearts.'

'And so you decided to take him away from me?' Edie's voice cracked.

'Not right away,' Lara said. 'At first, I was too taken aback. That first time I met you at the running club, I just kept waiting for the penny to drop. I kept waiting to see surprise in your eyes, shame in your face, but it never came. You just looked right through me. You stood there, smiling your dumb smile . . .'

On the line, Edie heard a rumbling sound, like a train passing, and Lara's voice was lost for a moment. 'You ruined my life and then you forgot all about me, didn't you? And then, later, I met your husband, and he didn't remember me either. It was like that whole thing had never happened, like Louise – that poor, naive, friendless girl – had never even existed. So I decided that maybe it was time to remind you.'

'And so . . . you *seduced* him?'

Lara laughed. 'Oh, that got to you, didn't it? That's what's bothering you! Not that I killed him, not that I bashed his brains out, but that I slept with him.' That cruel laugh again. 'You really are vain, aren't you, Edie? Well, set your mind at rest. I didn't sleep with him. I made him think that I might. But' – she made a little sound of disgust – 'he wasn't exactly the most

attractive prospect, was he? Broke, a fa.
moping over his awful wife, who was abou.
run off with his best friend . . .'

'Don't you dare talk about Jake like that,
don't you *dare*—'

'Why, Edie? Why shouldn't I call him a failure? It's what *you* called him, isn't it?'

Edie winced. 'I was not about to run off. I
would never have left Jake.'

'What are you talking about? You already had
left him!'

'It wasn't *for ever*. We were just going through
a bad patch. I would have gone back . . .'

'Because you loved him so much, or because
Ryan wouldn't have you?' Lara asked. 'I'm not
sure Jake would have had you back anyway. Do
you know, when I planted the seed in Jake's
mind – about you and Ryan – I expected to have
to work a little harder. But he believed everything. When I told him you hardly ever turned
up for running, Jake believed it. When I told
him you talked about Ryan all the time, he
believed that too. Every horrible thing I said
about you, he lapped it up. I was never sure why
he didn't try to defend you. Was it because he
didn't love you? Or because he felt so guilty
about what you and he had done to me?'

For an instant, a flash of lightning lit up the

die shrank down under her duvet. 'Are
saying Jake worked it out? Are you saying
knew who you were?'

'He was never quite so blinkered as you, was
he? After that half-marathon last year, do you
remember, I came out to the house? We were
drinking wine outside and there were all those
midges. You went inside to get some spray, and
I caught him staring at me. I thought he was
about to make a pass. But then, there it was –
this look of horror on his face. Horror and
shame. Finally! He WhatsApped me a couple of
days later, saying he wanted to talk. We met in
the Balmoral bar. He sat there, drinking and
sunk in self-pity, begging forgiveness . . .'

'I don't believe this!' Edie suddenly found
herself shouting into the dark. 'I don't! Jake did
not rape you, Lara . . .'

'No,' Lara said, her voice low and hoarse now,
like the voice in the story. 'You're right. Jake
didn't rape me. But he was in the room when
Ryan did.'

There was a strange noise on the line, a hiss-
ing sound, and then the phone went dead.

16

Edie had a swooping, sinking feeling in her stomach. She cringed, squeezing her eyes tightly shut. In her mind's eye, she saw a camera. She heard Ryan's voice, softly pleading with her. *Louise is saying we attacked her, we did stuff to her. We could be in real trouble*. She saw Jake, turning his face away from her.

They were all drunk. Before they even got to the party, they'd been drinking. Edie had nicked a bottle of vodka from her parents' drinks cupboard. And they were drinking it in the TV room, all three of them squeezed on to the sofa, watching music videos.

Ryan, who was messing around with the camera he'd been given for his birthday, wanted to go to the party. Edie would have preferred the three of them to stay at Jake's house. She and Jake had been going out for two months now. It was new and exciting, but nothing was as exciting as the feeling she got when she caught Ryan watching them. Watching *her*. But

efinitely wanted to go to the party, and
idn't want to be a downer – or worse, get
behind. So off they went, weaving along
e dark lanes on their bikes. Jake almost
crashed into a ditch at one point. She and Ryan
laughed at him, calling him a lightweight.

The party was being thrown by someone in
her year, someone with money whose parents
were away. When they arrived, everyone ignored
them. Everyone except for *Povvo*, who came
bouncing up right away, bra-less in her white
T-shirt, thrusting herself at Ryan. Edie remembered that part clearly. How Ryan smiled at
Louise. How he laughed with her. How he
offered her a swig from the bottle Edie had
brought. How she pressed her pink lips against
the bottle rim. She watched Louise and Ryan.
She felt Jake watching her, and she felt that the
whole evening was soured. She wanted to go
home. She walked off towards the kitchen, leaving the boys with Louise. She glanced back over
her shoulder to see whether one or the other
would follow her. Neither did.

Later, after an agonizing hour of standing
with her back pressed to the kitchen wall, hoping for someone – *anyone* – to talk to her, Edie
went back to find the boys. She walked through
the living room, and from there to a study.

From there she saw them, through the windo[w] out on the lawn. She thought for a momen[t] they were going home, leaving her behind, and she hurried out through the French doors on to a terrace.

Now she could hear them shouting at each other, she realized they were arguing. She felt a sharp sting of adrenaline: something was happening, something *exciting*. She saw Ryan grab hold of Jake's jacket collar, saw Jake wrestle himself away. She was trying to hear what they were saying to each other, but there was something else, another noise. She turned and saw a girl sitting on the floor, in the corner of the verandah, skirt hitched up to her hips, knickers showing, sobbing as though her heart would break. Edie took a step towards her and the girl looked up. It was Louise, her big blue eyes filled with tears, mascara streaking her pretty face. Edie turned away. She watched as Jake grabbed Ryan's camera from his hands and hurled it to the ground.

Edie's phone was ringing again. 'I thought I'd lost you,' Lara said when she answered.

'I didn't *know*,' Edie said, 'what happened at the party. How could I? I wasn't *there*. I wasn't in the room when . . . whatever it is you say happened . . .'

'But you said that you did know what happened. Or rather, you said you knew that *nothing* happened, because they were never alone with me. You lied.'

'I couldn't know for sure . . .' Edie was interrupted by a blinding flash, a fork of lightning striking alarmingly close. She gasped in fright. On the line, Lara did too. And then there came an almighty crash of thunder, a boom to shake the whole house. And Edie realized that she had not only heard it in the room, she had heard it *on the phone*.

She looked up. Through the darkness she could just make out the shape of the curtain, billowing as though caught by the wind. She heard the sound of the waves crashing against the cliff outside. She suddenly felt very cold, and sensed that it was not just fear chilling her to the bone. It was a bitter blast of cold air. Someone had opened the door.

Someone was in the house.

Lightheaded with terror, phone clutched tightly in her hand, she began to move towards the bedroom door. She pushed it open and peered along the corridor. Around her, the darkness thickened, solid and dense.

'Lara?' she called out. 'Is that you?' The sound of fear in her own voice made her more frightened still. She inched a little furthe. ward, feeling her way along the corridor know you're here.'

When she reached the doorway to the living room, she could see that there was a puddle of water on the floor in front of the sliding doors where the rain was coming in. Stifling a sob, she started to dial the police. She was on the second nine when she felt something in the air change – someone lunged at her, a shadow. She lurched backwards, but she was too late; the intruder was upon her, grabbing her arm and wrenching it behind her. Edie screamed as she dropped the phone. She felt something hit her on the back of her head, and she fell to her knees, crying out in pain.

17

The pain in Edie's head was unlike anything she'd ever felt before, sharp and intense at the back of her skull, blooming at the front into a tight, throbbing sensation. It was as though someone had placed a vice around her temples and was turning the screw. Her shoulder felt as if it had been wrenched out of its socket. She tried to move to ease the pain, but found that her hands were tied behind her back. When she raised her head, she saw her own face reflected back at her, her eyes black against the pallor of her cheeks.

The light was on. She was sitting on one of the dining-room chairs, facing the sliding doors, which were now closed. Slowly, she turned her head this way and that, but she couldn't see anyone. She couldn't hear anyone either, and the storm seemed to have died down. The only sound in the room was her own ragged breathing.

Then, from behind her, something else. A *yawn*.

'Are you awake?' Edie heard the click of ɪ on the concrete floor. 'You've been out fo while. I thought I was going to have to shaᴋ you.' From the edge of her vision, a shape appeared. Lara. She crouched down at Edie's side so that their eyes were level. 'How are you feeling?' she asked, wrinkling her nose. 'You look *terrible*. Would you like some water?'

Without waiting for an answer, Lara stood up and clacked off into the kitchen. Edie heard the tap turning on and off, and a moment later Lara stood in front of her, pressing the cool glass against her lips. Edie sipped and swallowed. A little of the water ran down her chin.

Lara scraped a chair across the floor and placed it in front of Edie's. She sat, rolling her shoulders back as she did, tipping her head from one side to the other as though she were warming up for a run. Or for a fight. She glanced back over her shoulder. 'Storm's blown itself out, I think.' Edie said nothing. She closed her eyes against the light. 'Funny how we ended up here, isn't it?'

'What? You mean with me tied to a chair?'

Lara chuckled. 'No, I mean up *here*. In Scotland. A long way from sunny Sussex.' Edie heard a familiar click and a hiss and she opened her eyes. Lara was lighting a cigarette. She smiled at

'You don't mind, do you?' Edie glared in response. 'Why *did* you come here anyway?'

Edie inhaled a lungful of Lara's smoke and started to cough. Lara rolled her eyes, waving the smoke away with her free hand.

'We moved because of the house,' Edie said. 'You know that. We had no money. We couldn't afford anywhere in London. Jake wasn't getting any work, and then his dad died. I told you this . . .' She started to cough again, the smoke catching right at the base of her throat. Lara sucked her teeth, dropped the cigarette on the floor and squashed it under the heel of her boot. She picked up the water glass and offered it to Edie once more.

'What about Ryan?' she asked, after Edie had taken a sip. 'When did he follow you up here?'

Edie regarded Lara through narrowed eyes. 'He didn't *follow* us. He got a good job offer, so he moved.'

Lara gave a little bark of laughter. 'Really? He was working in the City of London and decided to come to Edinburgh because that's where the big venture-capital action is? Are you really that stupid? Or is this just another example of you seeing what you want to see? Jake said Ryan followed you.'

'He did not.'

'Jake said Ryan followed you here beca[...] needed you. Because he needed someon[...] worship him the way you did. Because h[...] never met anyone in his adult life who did tha[...] People saw through his slick, surface charm. They saw him for what he was. A bully and a narcissist.'

'That's complete rubbish . . .'

'Is it? Didn't you ever wonder why Ryan never stayed in a job for more than a year at a time? Why his girlfriends never lasted more than a few months?' Lara sat back in her chair, the trace of a smile on her lips. 'Oh. I see. You thought it was because all the time he was carrying a torch for you, didn't you? You thought it was because none of them measured up.'

Edie struggled in the chair. The pain in her shoulder was still acute, but it was nothing compared to the agony of sitting under Lara's sharp gaze.

'Do you remember Tania? Ryan's old girlfriend, from a few years back? Do you know why that one didn't last? I'll give you a clue – it wasn't because of you. It was because Ryan beat her up, choked her. Tania came to Jake for help – he told her to go to the police. She didn't, of course, because it was her word against his. And these days men can get away with almost

...ng in the name of rough sex. So she let it ...e walked away. The thing is, though, *Jake ...eved her*. That's when he decided he had to ...et away from Ryan for good. That's when he decided he had to get *you* away from Ryan for good.'

Edie shook her head and kept shaking it. 'No, this is not true. Jake would have told me . . .'

'Would he?' Lara cocked her head to one side. 'Why would he have told you? He'd learned long ago that you wouldn't have a word said against Ryan. Do you know what he told me? *All Ryan has to do is look her in the eye and give her a smile and she'll do whatever he asks. She'll always take his side.*'

Again, Edie thought of the Monday after the party, when they stood at the school gates, Ryan's eyes locked on hers. *You have to tell them, E. You have to tell them it's not true.* Jake, turning his head away. Jake and Ryan stopped talking after that, for months. Edie and Jake never spoke about what was going on between him and Ryan. Whenever Jake brought up the subject, Edie shut him down. *I don't want to know*, she told him, *it's between the two of you. I don't want to get caught in the middle.*

'You're wrong,' Edie said, fixing Lara with her coldest glare. 'I didn't *always* take his side. Until

you came along with your little story, I tho
Ryan was guilty of murder.'

Lara walked off towards the kitchen agai
her heels clack-clacking over the concrete floor.

'I was wrong, though, wasn't I?' Edie called
out after her. 'Ryan is innocent, just like Jake
was. Jake did *nothing* to you!'

'Nothing?' Lara appeared once more at her
side, grabbing her by the shoulder. As she
moved, Edie caught the glint of metal in her
hand, seconds before she felt a blade against her
throat. 'He knew,' Lara hissed in her ear. 'He
knew what Ryan did. He knew, and you did too.'

18

After the storm, calm. Dead calm.

It was still dark, but in the light thrown from the house, Edie could see a fine mist of rain falling. She sat on the chair, her hands behind her back, trying with all her might not to tremble, willing her teeth not to chatter, her body not to shake with fear. She could hear nothing but the sound of Lara's breath in her ear, feel nothing but cold metal against her throat.

'Admit it,' Lara whispered. 'Just admit that you knew what Ryan did. Admit it, and maybe I'll take pity on you.' Edie closed her eyes. She swallowed and felt the blade press more tightly against her neck. 'Jake admitted it,' Lara said. Edie gasped as she felt the metal scrape her skin and then, suddenly, the pressure was gone.

Edie opened her eyes, exhaling a lungful of breath. Lara was still outside Edie's field of vision, but Edie could feel her presence, just behind her, could imagine the blade in her hand.

'A couple of nights after you walked ou[t] him, Jake WhatsApped me again. He asked to come out and see him. I drove all the way ou[t] here to listen to his drunken apologies once more.' Lara's voice sounded husky, as though she were on the verge of tears. 'I asked him again why he didn't say anything at the time . . .' She paused for a moment, clearing her throat. 'He said he didn't want to ruin Ryan's life. They were only teenagers, weren't they, after all? And he was *so, so sorry*, but he knew that if he told the truth about what Ryan had done, you would never forgive him. He would lose you both. So out of loyalty to Ryan, and love for you, he ruined *my* life.'

Edie bit her lip, tears filling her eyes. That was Jake all over, wasn't it? Loyal to Ryan and devoted to her. That summed up what they were all about. They were special. Other people just didn't quite count so much. Other people didn't even come close! Jake may have lost sight of that at the end, but he'd known that once.

'Admit it, Edie,' Lara said again, but there was an edge to her voice now, from tiredness or stress. 'I just want to hear you tell the truth.'

Edie drew a deep breath. 'Say that I do. Say I admit everything you want me to. Then what? Then what happens, Lara? You don't have a way

ere. You want me to tell you what happens
.t? You go to prison. Either that or you have
get rid of me, the way you did Jake. Only you
don't have anyone to pin it on this time, do
you? Whatever happens, this ends badly for
you.'

Edie felt the blade at her throat again. 'Maybe
it'll be worth it,' Lara said softly. Edie closed her
eyes, biting down harder on her lower lip. 'Or
maybe,' Lara's voice rose, 'you and I can make a
deal. You apologize to me, you beg my forgiveness, you let me walk away . . .'

'Why?' Edie gasped, her whole body trembling, the metal against her throat slipping
lower, towards her collarbone. 'Why would I do
that?'

'For Ryan,' Lara said. She angled the blade
against Edie's neck and then pulled it away
sharply, just nicking the skin as she did so. Edie
yelped, wriggling against her restraints.

'What do you mean?' she cried out. 'What do
you mean, *for Ryan*?'

Lara walked around the chair and stood in
front of Edie, her hands behind her back. She
looked thoughtful. 'What if I told you I had a
piece of evidence that would throw enough
reasonable doubt into the case to stop the pros-
ecution getting a conviction? A video, for

112

example, that – while not showing the [...]
face – would prove that the real killer was [...]
itely smaller and slighter than Ryan Pearce[...]

Edie shook her head. 'You're *insane*, y[...]
know that? You kill my husband. You frame hi[...]
best friend. You tie me up and torture me. And
now you're telling me you're going to set Ryan
free? Do you think I'm stupid?'

Lara shrugged. 'I'll have got what I wanted.
I'll have heard you say what I've been waiting
for you to say for fifteen years. I'll have pun-
ished you. I'll have put you through hell, and
Ryan too. You won't forget me again.'

Lara turned to look at the sea, and as she did
so, Edie saw that in her hand she held a pair of
kitchen scissors. Kitchen scissors! As soon as she
saw them, Edie's fear began to drain away. Lara
wasn't going to kill her! You wouldn't cut someone's throat with scissors, not when there were
sharp knives available.

Beyond Lara, beyond the window and the
garden, Edie could make out the faintest line of
grey on the horizon. It was morning. She had
survived the night.

'Okay,' Edie said.

'Okay?' Lara turned and stepped towards her,
the scissors gripped tightly in her right hand.

'Okay,' Edie said, raising her chin, exposing

...at in defiance. 'I'll take your deal.' Edie
...o intention of taking Lara's 'deal', but she
...sure now that Lara wasn't going to kill her.
...e was certain that, despite all her careful
planning, Lara didn't have a way out. Edie knew
that she was going to win.

'Can we go outside?' she asked. 'Please? I'm
in a lot of pain. I'll answer your questions. Only
let me get up off this chair and walk around,
please?'

Lara looked her up and down, taking in her
flimsy clothing, her tatty Ugg boots. She looked
back at the darkness outside. She was working
things out. She was betting that Edie wouldn't
be able to run away, not dressed like that, not in
this light. But Lara didn't know how well Edie
knew these woods, how well she knew these
trails. How, after the past few months, she
might just be able to find the shortcut through
the trees to the road, despite the dark.

Edie held her breath. 'Please?' she asked again.

Lara nodded curtly. She rounded the chair
and snipped through the cable ties securing
Edie's hands. Edie fell forward, hunched over.
The searing pain in her shoulder seemed to get
much worse before she felt a vast flood of relief.
She folded over, hugging her knees, releasing
the tension in her back. She rested for a second

before Lara grabbed hold of her arm, pul[...] her roughly to her feet.

Outside, it was very cold, the air filled wit[.] moisture. They stood side by side on the patio, their breath steaming, and, for a moment, they might almost have been friends again. Lara let go of Edie's arm. She stepped off the patio, teetering a little as her heels sank into the lawn. She took a few steps towards the cliff. In her hand, she still held the scissors, their bright orange handles like a beacon in the grey light.

Edie glanced over her shoulder. If she went through the house, she could lock the front door behind her, buy a little time. But she should wait. The more light there was, the better her chances of getting away.

'How did you know?' she asked Lara. 'That I had listened to your story, that I had seen the pictures of you on Jake's computer. How did you know all that?'

Lara turned to face her, her hair blowing across her face. She pushed it away. 'Before I set up this business, I worked in IT for years. I know everything about spyware. Took me about five minutes to get it on to your phone, on to your computer, on to Jake's, too. Since I visited your house the first time, I've had access to every stroke of every key, every number you dialled,

y app you opened. All this time, I've been
ching, waiting for my moment.'

She turned away, taking another step towards
the cliff. 'When it was over,' Lara said, 'I climbed
down there.' She pointed over the edge of the
cliff. 'The tide was out. I ran along the beach, all
the way to the headland.' Edie took a few steps
towards her. The waterlogged lawn squelched
beneath her boots, freezing water seeping
through their fabric. 'I washed his blood off in
the sea,' Lara said, 'and then I climbed back up
on to the path.'

She was talking about Jake. 'Did you feel anything?' Edie asked. 'Anything at all?'

In the half-light, she saw Lara turn towards
her. She could just about make out the shape of
her body, the whites of her eyes. 'I felt sorry,' Lara
said. 'And I felt frightened. I thought, I've done it
now. I've ruined my life. *Again*. And I shouldn't
have had to ruin my life again. I shouldn't have
had to waste myself on this. But what else could
I do? Once I'd seen you, I couldn't get you out of
my head. I couldn't stop thinking about what
you'd done to me, and how little it bothered
you, how little you must have thought of me.
How easily you looked away from my pain.
Because you thought you and your friends were
better than me, worth more than me.'

'We *were* worth more than you,' Edie snapped back. 'Still are. Always will be.' A surge of heat rose through her body, and she began to yell at the top of her voice. 'Did you really think I would beg your forgiveness? Do a *deal* with you? I'm not in the least bit sorry about what I did. I'd do exactly the same thing again. I didn't see anyone attack you. I didn't see anyone hurt you. Do you know what I saw? A messy drunk with her skirt hitched up around her knickers. A girl who'd worked her way through every boy in our class and had decided to move up to the next one. A girl who maybe got more than she bargained for.'

Lara's mouth gaped. She wept soundlessly. 'How can you say things like this? How can you be so blind?'

'I'm not blind at all!' Edie spat. 'I knew a line had been crossed. I guessed Ryan had crossed it. And I still chose him. I still chose *them*. Did you expect me to ruin my friendship with them for you? Just because you were a girl, I was supposed to take your side over theirs?' She shook her head. 'That sisterhood crap? I never bought it. I didn't side with you then and I wouldn't now. If I had my time again, I'd do exactly the same thing. I'd turn a blind eye.' She started towards Lara, hands curled into fists at her side.

d destroy you again and I wouldn't think wice about it.'

Lara made a noise. It sounded like a laugh or a cry, like one of the gulls. She stepped backwards and Edie saw her stumble, her heel catching in the soft ground. She tried to right herself, slipping sideways in the mud. The scissors flew from her hand as she fell on to her side, grabbing desperately at the grass as she tried to pull herself away from the cliff edge.

Edie lunged. She dropped to a crouch, snatching the scissors, lifting them and bringing them down, stabbing as hard as she could into the back of Lara's hand. Lara howled in agony, scrabbling away from Edie, dragging herself to her knees. She looked up at Edie, her face streaked with mud and tears, and Edie felt no pity, felt no mercy at all. She lunged once more, angling the scissors towards Lara's neck. Lara fell backwards, raising her arms to defend herself. Edie toppled too, the movement taking her forwards. Both of them were scrambling in the mud, trying desperately to get to their feet just as the ground beneath them started to give.

Epilogue

London, June
Eighteen months later

She couldn't hear herself think. Lights flashing before her eyes, blinding her. People waving, shouting, calling her name, voices coming from every direction: *Louise! Louise! Can you look this way, Louise?* She turned to one side, towards the loudest voice, almost stumbling over the hem of her gown as she did so. Her smile never faltered, not for a second. A dozen yards ahead, she saw Edie. She was wearing a short dress, black and sequinned, her runner's legs on show. People were shouting to her too, and she was smiling, showing lots of teeth. She glanced over her shoulder at Lara and winked.

(It wasn't really Edie, of course, just someone who looked a bit like Edie – a younger, prettier, more *alive* version of Edie.)

Eighteen months had passed since that morning on the cliff. Ryan was convicted of Jake's er. His claims about Jake's affair, for which could provide no proof whatsoever, were nored. His allegation that Edie's death was not suicide came across as paranoid fantasy. After all, Edie had sent an email message to Neeta Badami the morning she threw herself from the cliff. She had explained that she couldn't go on, that all the debt and the loneliness and the heartbreak were just too much for her to bear.

Bathed in the light and sound of a Leicester Square premiere, Not-Edie held out one beautifully manicured hand towards Lara (now also known as the screenwriter Louise Grant), beckoning her closer. Lara caught up with her and they embraced, kissing each other warmly on both cheeks. They entered the cinema together, hand in hand, passing together under the glowing sign proclaiming in letters large and bold:

WORLD PREMIERE: A Special Place in Hell.

About Quick Reads

"Reading is such an important building block for success"
- Jojo Moyes

Quick Reads are short books written by best-selling authors. They are perfect for regular readers and those who are still to discover the pleasure of reading.

Did you enjoy this Quick Read?
Tell us what you thought by filling in our short survey. Scan the QR code to go directly to the survey or visit
https://bit.ly/QuickReads2022
or scan the QR code

Turn over to find your next Quick Read...

A special thank you to Jojo Moyes for her generous donation and support of Quick Reads and to **Here Design**.

Quick Reads is part of The Reading Agency, a national charity tackling life's big challenges through the proven power of reading.

www.readingagency.org.uk
@readingagency   #QuickReads

The Reading Agency Ltd. Registered number: 3904882 (England & Wales)
Registered charity number: 1085443 (England & Wales)
Registered Office: 24 Bedford Row, London, WC1R 4EH
The Reading Agency is supported using public funding by Arts Council England.

Find your next Quick Read:
the 2022 series

Available to buy in paperback or ebook and
to borrow from your local library.

More from Quick Reads

For a complete list of titles and more information on
the authors and their books visit

www.readingagency.org.uk/quickreads

Continue your reading journey

The Reading Agency is here to help keep you and your family reading:

Challenge yourself to complete six reads
by taking part in **Reading Ahead**
at your local library, college or workplace
readingahead.org.uk

Join **Reading Groups for Everyone** to find a
reading group and discover new books
readinggroups.org.uk

Celebrate reading on **World Book Night**
every year on 23 April
worldbooknight.org

Read with your family as part of the
Summer Reading Challenge
at your local library
summerreadingchallenge.org.uk

For more information, please visit our website:
readingagency.org.uk